ANITA DESAI (née Mazumdar) was born in 1937 in Mussorie, India, to a German mother and an Indian father. She grew up in Delhi, speaking English, Hindi and Urdu, and published her first story at the age of nine.

Desai made her debut as a novelist in 1963 with *Cry, The Peacock* and followed it up with *Voices In The City* (both in Orient Paperbacks). Honoured with numerous awards, *Fasting, Feasting* is the third of her works to be short-listed for Booker Prize. She writes in English saying, 'I first learnt English when I went to school. It was the first language I learned to read and write, so it became my literary language.'

Most of her novels are set in India and completely immersed in Indian life. Prof Alan Lightman of Writing & Humanistic Studies, MIT, comments, '...her novels are distinguished by her focus on the inner life of her characters and her concern with people previously marginalised in Indian fiction, primarily women, children and the elderly.'

'The author has a deep understanding of human emotions. The characters come alive in the novelist's skilled hands.'

Indian Express

By the same author in

Orient Paperbacks

Cry, the Peacock

Voices in the City

Bye Bye, Blackbird

Where Shall We Go This Summer?

Anita Desai

Orient Paperbacks

DELHI | MUMBAI

For Ashwin

Acknowledgements

The poem quoted on pages 142 is *Che Fece... Il Gran Rifiuto* by G.P. Cavafy, translated by Rae Dalven.
The verse quoted on page 153 is from *End of Another Home Holiday* by D.H. Lawrence

www.orientpaperbacks.com
ISBN : 978-81-222-0088-1
Where Shall We Go This Summer?

Subject: Fiction

1st Published 1982
This Printing 2026

Published by
Orient Paperbacks
(A division of Vision Books Pvt. Ltd.)
5A/8 Ansari Road, New Delhi-110 002

Cover design by Sandip Sinha for Vision Studio
Printed and bound at TACT Printers, New Delhi

part one

monsoon '67

Moses waited. Waiting was what he did most of his time: it was not only his prime but also his legitimate occupation. So, with some righteousness in the lift of his heavy chin, he left the shallow dinghy to loll on the muddy waves, leaving his own monumental patience behind on the narrow seat to guard the oars, and wrapping his brilliant *lungi* more closely, more attractively about his hips, went into the tea shop on the beach to which a transistor radio allured him by its trilling songs, so ripe with sensuous promise. He sat amongst jars of pink biscuits and cream horns and calendars with lush mythological themes and drank sweet tea out of a thick glass. He was served respectfully — it is not everyone who is paid, has been paid for twenty years, merely for waiting.

He was not altogether comfortable, however. It was growing steadily hotter and muggier under the low, hammered-out, tin-can roof of the tea shop. The monsoon had temporarily withdrawn to the horizon, there to lie, visibly panting, collecting itself for another, stronger return, while on the land everyone waited — some with patience, some without — for the rain to begin again, and soon, with growing righteousness making his jaws ever heavier and stiffer and purpler. Moses rose and slipped through the back door of the shop into the smaller, darker, hotter precinct behind where only known and trusted customers such as

Moses were permitted and welcomed. This was the domain of the tea shop owner's wife, Jamila. She cackled to see him come and served him his favourite cashew nut spirits in a thick, smeared glass and stood scratching her head with a long hairpin as she watched him drink.

At first, he drank alone. Later, as the afternoon dwindled hopelessly into evening, neighbours of his from the island and some mainland men he did not know who had come to trade at the open-air market in Marve, joined him and his drinking quickened in pace and became almost jovial. Waiting lay less heavily on him.

'Hey Moses,' said Ali, the caretaker of the neighbouring house on the island. 'All dressed up for the market, are you?'

'Huh, the market,' Moses belched in contempt. 'Am I a trader? No, I am here on duty.'

'Drinking duty, eh?'

As they laughed, paying him back for his contempt, his eyeballs rolled like two porpoises making a brief appearance in the thick purple waves of his fleshy face. Then they sank soundlessly out of sight.

He remained silent, the others grew curious.

'Yes, that's a new *lungi,* isn't it?' remarked Joseph of the diesel-oil pump. 'And it isn't even time for the big fair in Bandra. That's when Moses usually goes gay.'

Moses gave the *lungi* a careless flick. Its checks of rose and maroon had about them the glow of square-cut gems —

therefore it was not only a careless but also a proud flick. 'I was sent twenty rupees,' he admitted. 'I had to spend it on something.'

'Twenty rupees! Who would send you a present like that — your mother-in-law?'

'My *memsahib!'* reared Moses suddenly, putting an end to the titters scampering around the table. 'The *memsahib* is coming.'

'No!' they all cried in disbelief.

'No one has come in twenty years,' said Ali, cruelly. 'No one will come now.'

'No?' roared Moses. 'Then why did she send me twenty rupees?' He nearly broke the glass as he slammed it down for emphasis.

'For a *lungi,* you said,' said Joseph, the careless sceptic.

'For preparing the house, getting it ready for her and her children.'

Then their voices took on some seriousness at last, even though the edges slipped into cups of cashew nut liquor.

'She hasn't come for twenty years,' repeated Ali. 'What would she want to come now for — after Moses has let almost the whole house fall down?'

Moses lifted the corner of his upper lip and snarled, showing teeth like mah-jong counters made of old bamboo.

'Perhaps that is what she is coming for,' cackled Jamila. 'She has heard that Moses has let the whole house fall down.'

'Who says the house has fallen down?' Moses bellowed, half-rising from the wooden bench on which they all sat. His bosom wore pendants of perspiration and their glitter seemed menacing in the ill-lit cavern of the illicit liquor shop. 'Show me one brick that has fallen,' he challenged.

'Many, many I will show you,' said Ali, drinking. 'Your wife has built a bathhouse out of the fallen bricks.'

Moses suddenly expanded — grew to the size of two, three Moses', each more purple, wet and gleaming than the other. The whole cavern reeked of Moses, was choked with Moses. His long growl was incoherent but not less threatening for that.

'For God's sake,' cried the tea shop owner, inserting his frightened face in a crack of the door. 'Jamila, keep order in there. Two policemen have come from Malad and are standing just outside the shop, drinking tea. They'll make me pay — they'll make me pay —.'

'Let the policemen come — let them come and count the bricks,' roared Moses, and the tea shop owner, a tubercular individual, hastily shut the door.

'Keep quiet, you, we can hear you all right, we are not deaf,' Jamila hissed at him. 'So, she is coming, the *memsahib.* Which one?'

'The younger daughter, of course,' Moses said, shrinking with mollification and at last sinking down on to the bench.

'The elder is too famous to come *here,'* he sighed and rescued his glass from the cluster on the table which was getting rather muddled.

'Ahh, the *younger,'* they sighed, turning into an audience again. 'Yes, yes, there was a younger daughter, too.'

'Of course there was,' spat Moses. 'Who has forgotten?'

'It was long ago they lived on Manori, Moses,' Jamila said, placatingly. She leant against the wall, raised one horny food and scratched it reminiscently. 'Our children won't even remember.'

'But we do, *we* do,' sang Joseph and Ali and several others, nodding their heads briskly up and down like so many goats neighing about the table.

'Who has forgotten the father?' Moses harangued them, but in a sing-song tone, ritualistic, almost dreamy.

'Not us, not us,' neighed the goats, wagging about the table.

Their neighing, Moses' growls, the sudden humming that had sprung up in their throats, together made a kind of music, like a religious chant, in that still, oily room in which the only lights were the sombre glimmers of Moses' magnificent *lungi.* Moses questioned them, the goats neighed their replies, and all seemed to sing, to hum together some mysterious, not wholly intelligible chant that belonged not so much to the Marve mainland with its tea shop, its diesel-oil pump, its illicit liquor and open market, but to the island,

Manori, there across the strip of sea, separate from them all, below the waiting, gathering monsoon.

'He rid my house of snakes and scorpions and no one was bitten again,' the words sang out, low but clear, from the centre of the massed, busy humming, as if produced by collective effort rather than individual inspiration.

'He made my wife bear who had been barren for twelve years, and she bore sons,' sang another in jubilant, astonished voice of one who has come to sing praise in a temple.

'He treated me for my fits and boils with powdered pearls and rubies and charged nothing,' praised a third in a voice of awe, as if laying offerings at an altar.

'I remember. Oh yes, yes, remember,' they all murmured, hummed, sang, and sank into shadows lumped on a wooden bench.

'Who has forgotten the well?' Moses roared to rouse them again, 'The only well in Manori that gives sweet water?'

'Ah, the well, the well. We remember. We know.'

'He dug it,' cried Moses, his voice unexpectedly high pitched and shrill. 'He drew water from it himself. He would not let me carry buckets for him. He went himself to the well, to fetch water for the house.'

'I can see him still,' sang Jamila, quavering by the wall. 'I can see him, all in white, as barefoot as us, on the rocks, going to fetch water.'

'It is sweet water,' they neighed. 'Sweet.'

'How fortunate the cow that drowned in it the other day. How sweet must have been her death,' sang Jamila, moving about them, refilling their glasses, touching them on the shoulders, reminding.

'Fortunate, fortunate,' they hummed and swayed and rocked.

Then one harsh voice, invisible, cried, 'But he died penniless — he left nothing,' and the twilight became rigid with a strange sense of disappointment — bitterness even.

Moses sank lower onto the bench, growing softer, darker, thicker. He nodded and he smiled and twisted, his face grotesquely as the religious music rocked him and entered into him, sweetly. He had served that man, he had looked after his house and well and trees, he had waited for twenty years. How sweet was such waiting, how rich, how whole and satisfying in itself! So he could not grasp immediately what had happened when the tea shop owner suddenly agitated the slats of the cracked door and hissed, 'They've come! They're here!' The words had to be repeated several times, more and more loudly, by all those caught in the cavern full of mysterious memories, before he rose unsteadily, wrapped the *lungi* about him closely, more limp and damp than it had been at the start, and lurched out to the tip of the Marve beach where a crowd had collected about a large car from the city, parked beside the hibiscus bushes.

They had not come out of the car — were unwilling to, it seemed, until Moses appeared and invited them to do so. He kicked aside the litter of yellow pups that lay sleeping in the dust and opened the door giving them one sultry look from beneath his eyelids then glancing away at once. The driver came out — dressed smartly in a khaki chauffeur's uniform stained between the shoulder blades with perspiration that somehow gave him added dignity — and, throwing up the lid of the boot, began taking out the luggage. It was a shabby hill of bags and boxes that grew there on the dust — not one piece looked smart, expensive or new. The gathered crowd gazed at it with some perplexity.

Then the woman came slowly, clumsily out of the back seat, sighing, shaking out the crumpled folds of her *sari* which was of some loose-woven material that seemed to be coming apart. She stood staring across the sea at the island which rocked and floated there like an aluminum bowl turned upside down, with eyes she shaded with one hand, and her face, too, was drawn up into a lined frown of perplexity. She had been a young girl when she lived on the island and Moses wondered that twenty years — twenty years that she had been so calm for him, and fruitful, swelling him out like some penduous jackfruit — had aged her so, turned her hair so grey. For a moment he wondered if she could be the daughter at all, the mistress of the house on the island — he had expected someone else, someone who had inherited the dignity, the mystery, and the ascetic splendour of the fabled father. She did not have it — had nothing, in fact, not even one piece of valuable luggage, seemed quite empty, vacant, stumbling. But she turned to speak to the children in the car with a certain terse crispness that brought them out. Moses had heard there were four children but only two appeared.

'And *Sahib*?' enquired Moses, peering again into the interior of the car as though it might, perhaps, hold another occupant who might prove more promising, more satisfying.

'No,' she said tersely and did not explain. She took the smaller child's hand and they fumbled down to the shore together. Moses watched them from under his eyelids and all his brave expectations, his concealed excitement, even the adventurous churn of the raw liquor ebbed from him: he felt only apprehension and shock.

'Chalo, chalo,' the driver was calling, he realized with a shock, to *him* — snapping his fingers with the insolence of a city man dealing with a yokel. *'Chalo,'* he shouted, 'get the luggage out. Isn't the boat ready?' to Moses who had served the father and waited twenty years.

With ponderous dignity Moses came forward and heaved the bags and boxes onto his shoulders and head — he was no city weakling to have to pick them up one by one, he was like a dusky ox who could be loaded and trusted. He staggered across to the boat, then stopped and shouted to the driver to come and unload him. The driver had no alternative but to come, dirtying his pointed shoes in the muddy ruts of the littoral, and help unload for the woman and children stood waiting.

As Moses handed them into the boat after the luggage — first the girl who held out a tentative hand with white fingers that did not grip, then the woman, and finally the small boy who let out a wail of fright as he found himself swung up into the air by the waist and then was quickly silent as he landed on his mother's lap — Moses was aware that all eyes were upon them, speculating, criticizing. The owner of the diesel-oil pump that catered to the few motor boats, came out of his shack under the coconut palms and stood picking his teeth with a match-stick, watching. Some of the Manori fishermen who had just brought in their craft with small hauls of fish for the market stood up in their battered boats and stared. The weekly market had begun to draw a crowd and this crowd, too, paused to watch the boat set out — women with their crimson and green *saris* tucked up between their legs and baskets of fish and small children on their hips, all stopped to stare. Then the ferry boat from the island chose that moment to arrive on the Marve beach and all those Manori fishermen bringing their dried Bombay ducks and green coconuts to the market and empty kerosene tins to be refilled, Marathi women in *saris* carrying baskets of custard-apples and Christian girls in stiff frocks bearing pink and yellow paper flowers for Marve church, all jumped from the ferry onto the beach and stood there, stuck in the sand and struck with wonder at seeing Moses with passengers and luggage in his boat.

Conscious of the thick concentration of attention on him, Moses waded luxuriantly into the sea, thigh-deep, pushing the boat before him. Then he flung himself into it with dramatic suddenness so that the boat tilted violently and the small boy bound himself frantically to his mother with the ends of her, *sari.* Calmly settling on the centre seat, Moses took up the oars and dipped them. The waves sucked down the oars, then released them. Casting a backward glance over his shoulder, Moses saw the audience on the shore stir to life, nudge each other and murmur. He lifted his pendulous jaw into the air and dipped the oars again, pulled at them with grand, dramatic gestures, feeling enlarged and solidified by his renewed duties, resolved to feel, if not proud (it was not possible to feel proud of a crew as tired, as lackadaisical and mundane as this) — then at least responsible.

❧

As the oars dipped into the sea and churned pools and ripples of motion in its turgid stillness, so the thrust of the boat from the shore and the beginning of the journey to the island roused something like motion in the woman who sat across from Moses. He saw her eyes start from her head so exaggeratedly that he was made to notice their immense size and extraordinary brilliance in that dry, worn face. Brushing her hair off her brow, she turned her head this way and that, her great eyes swallowing in the entire sea and the massed rocks and the palms of the island ahead of them — they were so large, so open, they could devour it all. Holding the child now with less intensity and easier emotion, she cried to him, 'We're off to the island, Karan, off to the island!' Shaking him a little, she bent her face to his, her eyes like huge lamps scanning his face, searching for response. 'Here we are in a boat, Karan,' she insisted, '*sailing* across the sea.'

'Where are the sails?' he asked, looking up at the sky, his pallid face reflecting the dullness of the late afternoon sky.

'It's only a rowing boat,' the daughter pointed out flatly, contemptuously. She sat hunched in the prow, her chin resting on her fist, staring at the mainland, staring at the people who had come to stare at them and now were turning to go about their errands, like ants who have paused, wondered, then gone on.

The woman cast a short, bewildered look at her, her face assuming the aged stillness that Moses could not relate, but only for a moment: she began restlessly turning, looking into the muddy sea as if to pierce its depth and discover its treasure, then at the island, then at the sky, as still and rigid as a boil slowly gathering to bursting point. Nudging the boy, she exclaimed, 'Look how dark the island looks against the sky, that shining white sky. See how exciting it looks!'

'Dark,' the boy whimpered, peering over her shoulder.

'Oh yes, it is so dark on the island. At night you see stars that you never can see in the city,' she assured him.

'But no lamps,' said her flat-voiced daughter.

'No lamps? *Of course* there will be lamps — real ones. Not electric bulbs but *real* lamps — lanterns. You'll see,' she cried, gathering her son and squeezing him again.

The boat, going at some speed now, cut a path through the sea and the foam fell apart and flew up at the prow. Turning to meet it, the woman bent low and dipped her arm into the sea.

'Don't, don't,' the boy screamed suddenly. 'There are snakes in the water!' and he pointed in horror at the strands of seaweed that the monsoon storms had uprooted from the sea-bed and which floated and tossed on the surface with the extravagant writhings of reptiles.

'Snakes!' the woman scoffed in exasperation — the child's imagination was perverse and pessimistic, she thought. 'Why, don't you see it is only weeds?' She reached out to catch a strand and show it to him, but Moses shouted, 'Sit still please *Memsahib,'* and she became rigid, staring at him as if she only now remembered his presence in the boat and wondered at it.

He lowered his eyes and concentrated on the oars, forced to abandon his observation of the family on account of her fixed scrutiny of his face. His jaws spread out and he looked sullen and rowed faster, dragging at the oars with great exaggeration. The children, too, studied him in silence. Unlike their mother, who continually broke apart into violent eruptions of emotion, the children seemed rigid, encased in their separate silences like larvae in stiff-spun cocoons.

But when Moses, lurching out of the boat onto the sand of Manori, the island, helped the girl out of the boat, she sprang onto the sand agilely and said, tossing the words at her mother with some cruelty, 'If there had been a storm, we wouldn't have been able to cross that bit,' and the boy, as Moses lifted him out of the prow and set him down beside his sister, agreed. 'Father *said* we would all be drowned,' he said with a sniff.

'How silly,' said their mother, very vexed, refusing Moses' hand and climbing down clumsily. He saw she was heavily pregnant. Her *sari* tumbled into the shallow sea and clung to her ankles, muddily. 'Is that why you were so frightened?'

'We were *not* frightened,' the girl replied with cutting scorn, tossing the hair from her face and turning contemptuously around to face whatever the island might present.

Moses, going back into the boat to heave out the luggage, was perplexed, not making anything of the tone of their voices. Their language he could not follow at all but he had expected the tone of their conversation to give him a lead and inform him why they had come. It gave him none — except that there were rifts and dissensions in the family as he had known there would be, must be, since there was no father to hold them together and lead them in obedience, nor even a husband.

The island offered them, to begin with, a lone soda-water shop under a clump of toddy palms and a very shabby, broken bullock cart in front of it, the bullock bowing its head beneath the great wooden yoke. The red paint on its horns made the only patch of colour in a scene that seemed all the more sallow now that the everhanging sky was flowering into a sunset radiance — the piled clouds, with the sun setting somewhere within their hearts, lighted from within like lamps in the shape of artificial roses, casting a light of fluid gold across the western sky. Rowing across the strip of sea, the island had seemed a small, dark blot of foreign matter on the pale dun sheet of the sea. Now, as they stood in the dust, watching Moses lead the bullock cart with their luggage, all three wincing every time another bag was flung in and the bullock staggered and then steadied itself, the island on which they had arrived seemed flat, toneless, related to the muddy monsoon sea rather than to the sky and cloudscape which steadily grew more gorgeous and brilliant by the second. The woman's face twisted — with disappointment or dejection.

The soda-water shop owner sat in the doorway, watching, chewing tobacoo, spitting.

Then Moses climbed up into the driver's seat — it seemed he was to be everything to them, would do everything for them, row a boat, drive a bullock cart, conduct and convey them, above all criticize and mock them for their folly in having come. Obediently they climbed in. The boy began to chuckle, a little apprehensively, but prepared to enjoy this wholly novel ride. Grateful for that chuckle, his mother beamed into his face, immediately ready to conspire with him in his delight. Moses curled his lip at that: What would become of a child given so much and such varying attention? 'Hroo,' he yelped at the bullock, 'hroo, hroo!'

The bullock cart set off down the rutted road — all that remained of the road after so much monsoon had washed over it. They drove now through deep, long pools, and now ever hardened ruts of clay. The unevenness made the bullock stumble and heave, the cart totter and lurch, so that there were no two movements alike in motion or direction. Each threw them off by its total unexpectedness. When they were prepared to be thrown to the left, the cart dipped and nearly threw them backwards into the slush. When they threw themselves forward to right themselves, it rolled drunkenly to the right. They clutched at the floorboards, digging their fingers into the cracks for a hold, stuck their feet out against the slats, and their bones ached with the effort of keeping together. Only Moses rode the heave and swell of that ride like some monstrous porpoise that easily lifts and falls with the waves and is never tipped or turned. His massive buttocks, crimson-clad, spread themselves out on the boards and trembled — but were not displaced. The young girl glared at him with a ferocity a man would surely feel, as he casually beat the bullock across its jutting hip bones, dug his whip into the soft flesh between the legs and gripped and twisted its tail, but Moses did not feel it — his back was broad, his hide was thick, it yielded only perspiration. The boy laughed and cried together, almost hysterically in pain and terror that did not quite obliterate the excitement of the adventure.

The woman, clinging now to the children, now to the cart, seemed to an irresponsible degree careless of the effects of the ride on her own condition: she had eyes and thoughts only for the country-side through which they drunkenly rolled. It was not picturesque — that seemed to startle her; perhaps she had forgotten that. The fields were only pits of mud and slush. Whole shanty towns seemed built of bamboo stakes on which the Bombay duck was habitually hung to dry but now stood stark, only a forgotten fish or two still impaled on the stakes, left to rot. The Manori village was an evil mass of overflowing drains, gaping thatched roofs and mud huts all battered and awry. The villagers stared at her, she at them — at the children sitting amidst the pigs, as naked and muddy as they, at women squatting in the thick smoke of damp fires, and men slack with monsoon idleness. All knew Moses and had called to him as he had set out that morning, but none spoke to him now — they stared at his passengers and held their tongues.

The village pond, an artificial tank with broken stone steps, was full to the brim and could be differentiated from the pools and puddles of the fields only because its water was not brown with mud but green as spinach, thick, viscous. The woman disregarded its filth, its solid green layer of germs and disease, and thought it beautiful, for there were women closely wrapped in *saris* of scarlet and crimson on the stone steps, dipping narrow-necked vessels of brass into it and squatting beside it to wash and beat mounds of coloured clothes with that crude, dark vigour of the Bombay fisherfolk. One muscular woman with an aubergine skin, wearing a mango-green *sari,* stood up and was the first on the island to hail them. She yelled to the other women, they paused — one with a brass vessel half-lowered from her head, another knee-deep in the spinach-water pulling at some sugar-pink water lilies, a third with her arms plunged into a mound of soapy washing. They laughed, hooted, white teeth and red gums like newly-opened gashes in their faces, and called out to Moses in voices that rang like jeers or taunts. Behind them was a grove of mango trees, their leaves in dark and glittering, and a flash of phospherescent parrots suddenly shot out of them like so many rockets at a carnival, then sped into a sky of rose and orange, shrieking.

It was a brilliant scene, each of its colours enamelled upon the gold of the background. Yet — as if to prove it had no reality, no substance, was no more than a painting, an enamelling, open to interpretation — when the woman said, 'How beautiful, look, how beautiful,' her daughter pinched her nostrils and said, 'Oh will they really *drink* that stinking water?' which made the woman sigh reflectively and turn away from the vivid scene as the cart heaved itself up and climbed the incline to the paddy fields that lay, banana-fringed, above the village and its tank.

As they lurched along the road, the paddy fields on either side of them, filled with still water, drank in the sky and its light and reflected the brilliance of the sunset in a way that made it seem the bullock cart was breaking a path through a mirror, leaving a jagged black crack in the liquid sheen of sunset colours. It was at once an inspiring and frightening sensation — and the passengers of the cart seemed to crouch and droop, clinging to the shifting planks, almost afraid of the gorgeousness they were disturbing. They stared and watched as those depthless fields drank and swallowed, drank and swallowed, the liquid shades of gold, of sunlight, till all at once it was all gone. The sky and the water both turned to a toneless shade of pearl, then grey, then darkness.

The paddy fields came to an end. The cart gave a great lurch onto a knoll and then carried them at a suddenly brisk roll into the black shadows of great coconut grove.

Piling out onto the grassy knoll they saw trees rearing up about them like columns of darkness, their black fans closing together above them and only glimpses, at the foot of the trunks, of a sunset over the sea from which all the rich light was gone, leaving only the amber shades that glowed but gave no light.

Clumsily, feeling her hands impeded by the dense darkness pouring onto them from the trees, the woman was helping her son out, half-asleep, when the ghostly rustling and rattling of the palms were torn apart by a strident cackle, rasping and shrill, yowling in a tomcat's voice that reeled about with liquor fumes, 'A little baba for me! Ho, Moses, you have brought a little baba for me,' and Karan felt his face smacked with lips of alcohol-soaked rubber and let out a scream and a kick of terror.

It was Miriam, Moses' wife who matched him inch for inch in height and breadth and had, apparently, the same resources and habits of passing the time as he. Sita, recognizing her, said coldly, 'He is nearly asleep. Give him to me,' and took back her son. Miriam cackled and made pinching, snatching gestures at Karan's shrinking bottom, pursing up her lips and making wet, kissing sounds as she did so. Sita wrapped her arms around the child and carried him up the knoll, calling to the girl, 'Come, Menaka, the house is up here.'

'I can't see,' Menaka complained, stumbling in the knotted monsoon grass. 'There's no light.'

'Moses will light the lanterns. But you can still see the sky lit up.'

So they walked towards the sky which was a vast pink Japanese lantern swinging low over the sea in the great mass of surrounding darkness. The palms reared up in their path, hissing and clattering their dry leaves together harshly, like some disturbed, vigilant animals — stiff bats, sharp cranes or dire geese rather than trees, mere vegetables. There was menace in their warnings, and vigilance, also a certain promise.

Sita's feet seemed to remember, instinctively, the path that led through them, from Moses' small kingdom — his hut, his cattleshed, goat-house, chicken-pen and well — to the house at the top of the knoll. It was built on a high stone plinth, itself an island lapped by waves of palm and the shorter, quieter, leafier trees that grow to the height of its balustrade. Its white walls gleamed chalkily above the waves of this dark foliage and Sita took the children resolutely towards it — at least it stood. She took them round to the front of the house which faced the sea and a steep flight of stone stairs led them to a deep veranda with a balustrade and white pillars like so many painted, leafless palm trees.

Here she halted for the house was pitch dark. They would have to wait for the lanterns to be lit. 'Moses,' she called, looking over the balustrade into the palm forest, but there was no sign of him and they seemed to have shaken off and lost even the adhesive Miriam. She probably lay under some bush, sleeping the rancid, rattling sleep of the drunk. But Moses? 'Moses,' she called, and her daughter slumped down on the stone seat beneath the balustrade and her son seemed asleep on her shoulder — she was utterly limp. 'Moses, Moses,' she cried.

The only sounds were vegetable, salt-seasoned.

She decided to enter the rooms — the doors were all wide open and swung back and forth in the wind, idly crashing — and as she stepped in she realized the boy had not slept at all, had merely been paralyzed by fear of being pounced on and kissed by the nightmarish Miriam again, for now he stiffened on her arm so that he nearly slipped out of her hold and fell, wailing 'Dark! Dark!' He kicked and twisted and would not let her enter the dark house in search of a lantern or candle. She stood helplessly, feeling perspiration creep down her skull, her arms aching with his weight but unable to part with him or do anything with him.

So they stood despairingly in the deep veranda, the white doors of the house all swinging outwards, revealing the crowded darkness inside. Below them was the shifting, sighing darkness of the palm leaves leading down, she remembered, to the sand dunes and the sea. All the rose had faded out of the sky as from wet paper. A nest of bats somewhere close to them squeaked and the palm fronds slithered about them in the rising breeze.

Eventually Moses came, at his leisure having stopped for a smoke before unloading the cart and carrying the boxes up.

'Where are the lights?' cried Sita, frantic to put her son down and have a smoke herself. 'Everything is dark.'

'I have come to light the lamps,' he said easily, a little contemptuously.

'Why didn't Miriam?'

'*I* have the keys,' he said. Now that he had deposited them at the house to which they had come at no invitation from *him,* and there was no watchful audience any more, he seemed to have dropped his pretence of respect for them. He disdained them — that was very clear: the unworthy offspring of the illustrious and well-remembered father.

'*What* keys?' she asked passionately. 'The house is all open.'

'Ah, but the store is shut,' he said and disappeared into the house. Presently the first lamp was lit, then the second.

For a while they remained on the veranda, watching the slow, wavering bloom of light. Then she went in at last and saw what had become of the house in twenty years of absence — a waste of ashes she saw, the cold remains of the bonfire her father had lit here to a blaze. Ashes, white, and waste. Dust lay as casually as sand on a beach, spiderwebs spanned the corners of the unfurnished rooms like skeletal palm leaves. The odour was of bats and mildew, and silence boomed like the silence of undersea caves. It had no air of providing shelter from the sea or beach — it was as much a natural part of them as an abandoned shell or lump of twisted driftwood.

Moses squatted beside the lamps, proud of their flames, waiting, not without insolence, for the so-called mistress to deal with her home which he had handed back to her like the rusted but possibly useful key to the lock of — what? She had known, she thought, but now she saw she didn't.

So she spoke angrily. 'Why haven't you cleaned it?'

He rolled his eyeballs drolly. 'It will take much time to clean.'

'You *had* time. Why didn't you do it?'

His jaw swung — warningly, she saw — then rigidified into a purple barrier about his face. 'I've lit the lamps,' he said sulkily and, getting up, began to shuffle towards the door.

'Here!' she cried in a panic for her whole body ached with a shrill insistence and the thought flickered through her of the flat in Bombay, white with electric light, the twinkle of china, the meal served by servants in white, the routine to which the children were used, and their beds, smooth, cool. 'Bring the luggage in,' she ordered. 'Get the beds made. And food — haven't you got any food made?'

'What was I to cook?' he sulked.

'But I sent you money for it!'

'There is nothing to buy here. No fish in monsoon season.'

'No fish? Couldn't you have bought vegetables then, and milk for the children?'

He began to shuffle out more purposefully then.

'Come back!' she screamed. 'Come here. Where are you going?'

'To fetch milk,' he growled, then blended instantly with the darkness.

'Oh,' said Sita.

'We might at least have brought one servant with us,' Menaka said bitterly.

'Don't sulk,' Sita told her sharply and set the boy down on a string bed that resembled a tattered hammock. Her voice had such an edge, her movements so much force, that the child did not protest but let her go and unpack, make the beds, hunt for a packet of biscuits in one of their baskets. But he appealed to his sister with a mute roll of his eyes and she came and sat beside him, placing one hand on his knee. So they sat, in silence, hollow-eyed in the quavering shadows cast by the lantern, like a pair of owls, watching Sita drag the bags from one room to another, pull the two string beds together, unpack and tidy. Every time she caught their eyes, the accusation in them made her turn abruptly away, having no answers for them. Once she said, hysterically, '*Help* me.' Then they got up and stood around with the stunned faces of parcels, waiting for her to collect and deposit them, disbelieving utterly that this could be the right address.

Guilt wore her out. She finally sat down at the table and fed them biscuits and the milk Moses brought in a brass vessel, watched them nibble and sip in silence while she smoked a string of cigarettes. Stamping them under foot, she got them up, changed them, put them to bed with her last reserve of strength, moving already semi-consciously, like a zombie. She sat for a while at the edge of Karan's bed, smoking another cigarette, as though this last one may convey an assurance or an answer, then lay down at his side in a heap.

'Won't you even shut the doors?' Menaka asked from the other bed.

'Whatever for?' she asked and lay in a kind of paralysis, listening to the tide come in, the wind lift, the palms storm and lash till, before morning, the monsoon set in again with fully restored and renewed passion. Then her paralysis melted a bit, gave way, and she turned on her side, painfully, cut and gashed by the strings of that wrecked bed, and gathered the sleeping boy close to her, burrowing her face into the pillow beside his, breathing in his breath which smelt, like an infant's, of sugar, cradling his small hips in the crook of her arm, edging closer to him, away from the wild season around them, and slept.

She had come here in order not to give birth. An explanation she had repeated to herself and her husband so often that, instead of acquiring lucidity — 'Ah! Oh, *now* I understand!' — it seemed steadily more strange, mistaken. Yet she had arrived, she was on the island, in order to achieve the miracle of not giving birth. Wasn't this Manori, the island of miracles? Her father had made it an island of magic once, worked miracles of a kind. His legend was still here in this house — in the green tinge of the night shadows, the sudden slam of a wooden shutter, the crepitation of rain on the roof — and he might work another miracle, posthumously. She had come on a pilgrimage, to beg for the miracle of keeping her baby unborn.

She had had four childern with pride, with pleasure — sensual, emotional, Freudian, every kind of pleasure — with all the placid serenity that supposedly goes with pregnancy and parturition. Her husband was puzzled, therefore, when the fifth time she told him she was pregnant, she did so with a quite paranoiac show of rage, fear, and revolt. He stared at her with a distaste that told her it did not become her — a woman now in her forties, greying, aging, to behave with such a total lack of control. Control was an accomplishment that had slipped out of her hold, without his noticing it, over the years, till now she had no more than an infant has, before he has begun the process of acquiring it, and so she wept and flung herself about, over-forty, grey and aging.

'But you were always so pleased about the babies, Sita,' he said, closing his fists, unclosing them, uncertainly. 'They always pleased you.'

'I'm *not* pleased, I'm frightened,' she hissed through her teeth. *'Frightened.'*

'Why? Why?' he spoke gently. 'Everything will go well. I thought it grows easier and easier.'

'It's not easier. It's harder — harder. It's unbearable,' she wept.

So it continued through the sick, curtained, reclining months. He hoped — standing in the doorway, closing his fists, unclosing them — that once the discomfort and physical misery were over, she would fill again into that comfortable frame of large, placid joy, of glazed satisfaction, of totally inturned pride and regard, as she did usually, as did other women one saw pacing with a measure that would be majestic were it not a little vainglorious. But she filled out little, she did not strut, she did not acquire the stretched skin and the lustre he waited for — she continued to huddle, to twist her fingers, to smoke bitterly through the nights and display an agony that he felt was as unbecoming to her as it was puzzling to him.

The day he remarked, 'Not much longer to go now, Sita, it'll soon be over,' the storm broke. All through their married life they had preferred to avoid a confrontation. All that they had done, he now saw, was to pile on the fury till now when it exploded. Perhaps there had been incidents, thoughts during the day he had not known about, would have left undisturbed had he known. It was as though for seven months she had collected inside her all her resentments, her fears, her rages, and now she flung them outward, flung them from her.

Tossing clothes, cigarettes, books into the suitcase that she had dragged down from the tops of cupboards, she was silent and blind in the face of his alarm and disbelief as he stood watching and not quite believing what he saw. It was an expression that was not infrequently fitted on to his face. Now and then he exclaimed, 'Don't be silly,' and 'Sita, don't behave like a fool,' and 'Think of your condition.'

'What do you know about my condition?' she flared. 'I've told you — I've tried to tell you but you haven't understood a thing,' and hurled slippers, papers, nightgowns.

'I don't understand much, but I understand you are having a baby and must not be allowed to behave like this. You *must* stay where there is a doctor, a hospital, and a telephone. You can't go to the island in the middle of the monsoon. You can't have a baby there.'

'But I don't *want* to have the baby,' she cried. 'I've told you.'

His face, usually as stolid as soundly locked gate, receded half an inch in shock. It was not only the brutality, the murderousness of this statement that seemed to attack him with the clubs and spears of a beastial civilization, but it seemed so shockingly out of character with a woman who had once stood all day on the balcony, keeping away the crows that were attacking a wounded eagle on a neighbouring roof top, and who winced dreadfully every time she heard a child cry. The shock made him unsteady on his large, well-shod feet. He swayed a bit. 'It's too late to do that,' he said with thin lips that were glued together at the corners. It was true he had laughed at her for acting the scarecrow over the half-dead eagle, but — all the same — he revered life. He had not read the *Vedas* or the *Mahabharata,* nothing more than scattered verses from the *Bhagvad Gita* — still, he was born a Hindu. Family planning was all very well, but not — 'You should have thought of it earlier,' he said. 'It's too late now.'

'Too late? Why too late? It's not born yet.'

He was repelled, he turned away, not being able to see her any more for hatred of her. He hated her, hated her talk. 'One can't have an abortion at this stage,' he said fiercely, his face turned aside.

'Hu —' a breath fell from her heavily like a stone dropped, 'Wh — what?' she stammered. 'Wh — abortion?'

They stared, uncomprehendingly, at each other, more divided than they had been on the balcony that day — she fighting, the other laughing. What did he mean? What did she mean? In that snarled moment of silence, time was a scummy sea, telling nothing.

'What do you mean — abortion?' she gasped, her eyes burning.

'I suppose that's what you mean — you want one.'

'Mad!' she gasped. 'You're quite mad. *Kill* the baby? It's all I want. I want to *keep* it, don't you *understand?*'

'No,' he shouted in exasperation, feeling himself made a fool that she spun round and round her finger till he was sick and giddy. 'You just said you don't want it. Now you say you do want it. What's up? What's up?'

'I mean I want to *keep* it — I don't want it to be born.'

'Mad,' he breathed in relief, understanding all in a stumbling access of clarity. He saw her again as she had stood, on the balcony, in the glitter of afternoon light, holding her son's popgun, its cork dangling from its mouth, absurdly: the intensity of that attitude was now explained. 'You've gone mad.'

'I think,' she said, going back to the suitcase and the filling of it, 'what I'm doing is trying to escape from the madness *here,* escape to a place where it might be possible to be sane again.'

'*Who* is mad here? In this house? What madness?' and he gestured towards the door that led into the bedroom where the children slept and the servants quiety tidied up and put away and locked up for the night. 'What madness is there *here?'* he asked, loudly, righteously, pointing to the familiar patterns, the quiet regularity carefully arranged outside their bedroom door — so carefully arranged by him.

'It's all a madness — the boys acting out that scene from the film they saw, fighting each other on the floor; Menaka and her magazines and the way she's torn all those drawings of her's I'd kept so carefully; the *ayah* taking Karan to that — that roadside dump where all the *ayahs* sit and gossip and fight; the way you laughed because I tried to keep the bird alive; the people here all around us, living here, all *around....*' she stopped too distressed to continue.

He found her unbearable in her distress, the drama of her distress. He was still closing and unclosing his fists unconsciously, but he strained to speak more lightly. 'So you're running away — like the bored runaway wife in — in a film.'

She stabbed him between the temples with a short, ferocious glare. 'It can happen in real life, Raman,' she said. 'I will go. I am leaving tomorrow. On the island — it'll be different.'

He laughed, drawing in his breath so sharply that his nostrils whitened. 'You want to work a miracle,' he mocked. 'An immaculate conception in reverse.'

'Why not?' she challenged with a bravado that came to her too easily once she was astride an idea, skimming on it, floating. She had kept that bravado alive, afloat through that sleepless night and the following day, the kidnapping of her one daughter and the youngest son, the long drive through the slums in the heat that poured down like molten lead, the boat ride across the monsoon sea, even the nightmare arrival at the old house on the once magic island, to find the past all burnt to white ashes. Only now it failed her as she awakened after the initial spell of thoughtless sleep at Karan's side on the string bed.

From the depths of her memory she brought out a poem of Cavafy's that she kept there like an amulet, etched on the dull metal of her mind, and that she drew out and fondled when she was afraid:

To certain people there comes a day
    when they must say the great Yes or the great No.
He who has the Yes ready within him
    reveals himself at once, and saying it he crosses over
        to the path of honour and his own conviction.
He who refuses does not repent. Should he be asked again,
    he would say No again. And yet that No —
        the right No — crushes him for the rest of his life.

He had been certain she would be crushed, had not believed it could be otherwise. Seeing her climb on to the chair again and hurl down a second suitcase off the top of the cupboard, he had said in a bewildered way, 'But you're not leaving for such small incidents, Sita? They occur in everyone's life, all the time. If you are an adult you know how to cope with them — they are only *small* incidents.'

One small incident.

Crows formed the shadow civilization in that city of flats and alleys. She watched them from the balcony, hopping clownishly about the rocks on which the sea broke, scrambling to catch a rotten fish or scraps of edible flotsam left by the waves to stink in the sun. They even sat on the ledges and balcony rails of the flats, waiting for lazy cooks to throw out a bucketful of kitchen garbage into the alley — scraps were caught by them in mid-air, expert for all their clownishness, tattered wings holding them aloft as they twisted and flapped to get the largest bits. There was always much black drama in this crow theatre — murder, infanticide, incest, theft, and robbery, all were much practised by these rough, raucous, rasping tatterdemalions.

It took her some time, therefore, to realize that Saturday morning as she sat helping her older sons with their geometry, that it was an exceptionally cruel drama that had aroused the crow world outside and made them churn the air, joyously screeching, then alash with rapacious claws and beaks at something that lay struggling in a mound of rust on the ledge that jutted out below their balcony.

Leaning far out over the rails she made out, after a while — dazzled by the crumpled aluminium foil glitter of the morning — that the tortured creature cowering unshaded in that sun was an eagle, wounded or else too young to fly.

With glee the crows whistled — *whee;* in ecstasy they waved their wings; *crra-crra,* they laughed and rasped as they whipped it with their blue-bottle wings and tore into it with their scimitar beaks. It rose weakly, tried to crawl into the shelter of the wall's shadow and its wings, leaf-red, scraped the concrete, then its head, gold-beaked, fell to one side.

Sita shouted for her sons. Then she shouted for stones.

'From downstairs?' they shouted, panting, ready to tear downstairs for some. But that would take too long. 'A stick,' she decided instead.

They found the long-handled brush with which the ceilings were, at intervals, swept. They swung it head-down, clattered it against the rails, but with no effect — the crows were used to a certain amount of opposition and aggression from the human population of the city; they could tackle it, ignore it, choking with laughter. A group of three fell on the eagle together. It struck out with its effete wings and the crows shot upwards, like witches speeding skywards, and beakfuls of soft breast feathers fluttered down.

'Get a gun,' Sita shouted desperately, flinging down the brush.

'We don't *have* a gun,' the eldest boy reminded her bitterly. His best friend had one — he had often told her that, meaningfully. No, she had said firmly — and now she wanted a gun.

'The toy gun. Go, Karan, the toy gun will do.'

The smallest child, awed at being chosen as the instrument of deliverance, ran for it so fast that he fell. He cut his chin and bawled but was ignored. She fetched it herself, out of his toy box. Shot it. Pop — out popped the absurd cork and dangled, smokeless. But the crows knew a gun when they saw one, knew it to be different from the foolish broom-stick. *Crra!* they screeched in surprise, flailing their wings and wheeling away. Tatterdemalions all in a tantivy. She laughed and shot at them again and again — *pop! pop! Whhoosh,* they whistled and shrieked, veering off to other buildings, to settle on other rails, shrugging their shoulders in disappointment. The eagle lay still.

'Do you think it's dead?' the boys asked.

'No, resting. Let's see if it flies away now.'

They watched. It did not move and the crows soon swept into attack once more. *Pop, pop,* she fixed the gun. *Crra, crra,* they cried, wheeling away, furious at this unaccountable barrage of shots keeping them away from their warm-blooded, waiting meal. But they had the persistence of the ignorant — if she could stand on the balcony fixing at them all day, then they could attempt, whenever she paused, to fly through the hail of pops and get at the eagle that lay so still that it was in all probability dead. 'No, it moved,' she shouted, shading her eyes against the dazzle of the sun on the sea. Karan, nursing his cut chin, came to hang over the rails and nodded, but the older boys, growing bored, claimed, 'It's dead,' and went into their room.

Menaka, coming home from a visit to a friend, stopped on the balcony to stare at the odd figure of her mother standing by the rails firing Karan's pop-gun at the furious band of crows. She watched for a while, in astonishment, then pressed her lips together and went away without asking for an explanation — her mother had before arranged, created wilfully such acts of drama purely, Menaka maintained, to embarrass her family. This, she thought, closing her bedroom door, was another.

In the evening, the tide sank, the sun sank, the littered rocks stank, and the crows flopped down onto the rocks, were quiet there, drowned in the booming purple sea. She put her pop-gun away.

In the morning there was nothing on the ledge but a drift of feathers, some fawn, some russet, and stains that might have been of blood. Crows sat complacently on the balcony rails, rooftops, window sills and rails. They leered at her, cawing conversationally.

'They've made a good job of your eagle,' said her husband, coming out with his morning cup of tea. 'Look at the feathers sticking out of that crow's beak,' he laughed.

'Perhaps it flew away?' she cried, knowing it had not.

❧

Another small incident.

At five o'clock in the afternoon, washed and dressed, Karan was sent with his *ayah* to play with the other children of the neighbourhood in a cul-de-sac just out of sight of Sita's balcony. There was no park nearby, not a patch of green anywhere, and the children, for all their neatly pressed cottons and pretty coloured shoes, played in the roadside dirt with their toy cars and trains, with pebbles and lumps of asphalt, while the *ayahs* gossiped and smoked, discussing their *memsahibs,* their lovers, and the cinema. Sita watched Rosie lead Karan decorously down the road, then sank into her chair for a second cup of tea and a cigarette, slowly smoked.

There was a sudden sound like the screeching of brakes, a commotion — only it was not a common road accident but a clash and clamour of aroused women. The *ayahs,* were up in arms. Hearing the screams, Sita leapt up to lean over the rails and peer down the street, and although she could not see the women fighting in the cul-de-sac, she could see the passers-by who had stopped to stare, and the whole street seemed to quiver and whip with their passion and rage. There was a clamour of shouts and accusations, screams and shrill, tooting sounds as the argument gave way to action. She thought she saw the madly flapping edge of the battle-scene — arms flailing, *saris* ripping. Certainly children were crying. Tea, book, cigarette — abandoning them, she ran.

Yes, children were crying out to the edge of the battle, yet not daring to leave their *ayahs* and run. The *ayahs* were warring — Goanese women, Mangaloreans, fisher folk turned city domestics, Bombay women, huge hipped, deep-thighed, pink-gummed and habitually raucous, they were pushing each other, then pulling, tearing each other's flowered frocks and pink and green *saris,* then dragging the rips together. All were bawling.

Sita pushed hysterically through a battery of them till she saw Karan standing with his head bowed to the blows flying above his head, his knees rubbing together his mouth wide open and tears trickling out of the corners of it. Snatching him up, she whirled around to find Rosie. Rosie was at the thickest knot of this loud fury — she was trying to pull herself free from two women who were trying to restrain her or overpower her, and bawl ing at a Marathi *ayah* who had her *sari* tucked up between her legs like one of her ancestral warrior-women prepared for battle. 'Rosie, come away,' Sita gasped but Rosie did not hear — she had her head thrown back and was screaming abuses in three languages, clearly either the heroine or the villain of the piece. Sita had to leave Karan at a safe distance outside the ring of turmoil, then go back and tug Rosie out of the knot, crying to the women to let her go, to go home, to be quiet. She dragged Rosie step by step out of the ring for Rosie stopped again and again to hurl one more abuse at the growling, wailing women. Then she snatched up Karan again and called to Rosie to follow. 'You *must* come,' she ordered her.

Upstairs in their flat, the door shut behind them. She knelt and examined Karan with shaking fingers, beginning to sob herself. There was a scratch on his leg. 'Who scratched you?' she cried, shaking him, shaking herself. 'Who scratched you here?'

'I was climbing the gate.' he said, calm now. 'It was poky.'

'Rosie, *who* scratched him?' Sita demanded, but Rosie had flounced off to the kitchen and was bawling out her story to the cook in Goanese. Sita following her, dragging Karan along by the hand, tried to interrupt her and halt the rushing, frothing flow of her talk with some furious questions. Rosie burst into tears at last and went howling to her room.

'It is like living in the wilds,' she said to her husband at night. 'One may be attacked — one's children may be attacked in the streets.'

Sensing the black cloud of her melodrama rising, his lips became glued at the ends, tightly. 'Karan said it was the poke of the railing that scratched him,' he reminded her.

'He doesn't know — he only says that. It could have been the women with their *beastly* dirty nails.'

'They were fighting with Rosie. Rosie started it — the cook says. Rosie is aggressive.'

'Yes, I know — but everyone is. Everyone fights. They are *all* violent.'

'Don't make too much of it — you'll upset Karan. Just tell Rosie not to go there again.' He closed his mouth, closed the incident. But she could not quietly pick up her book and read for nothing ever closed for her: ripped open, the wound remained open.

More small incidents.

Like the waves incessantly, tiresomely, crashing into each other, her sons hurled their bodies at each other as if they were made for attack and combat. She came upon them on the floor, one buckling the other beneath him, being overthrown, then both rolling, both enmeshed, thrashing, grunting. Her screams did nothing to stop them.

'They're only playing,' Menaka told her, censoriously enough but including her mother in her prim censure.

'That's no way of playing,' Sita said. 'Get up. Get *up.* Stop it.'

They stopped suddenly too, out of breath to strike another blow. She hated the sight of their red faces dripping, their chopped hair sticking in clumps with sweat. But they laughed. 'This is how they did it in the fil-um,' the younger said, surprised at her expression.

She came across the same look of surprise when she flew into kitchen, demanding, 'What's happened?' Interrupted, the cook and the *ayah* gazed at her and at each other. 'Nothing,' said the cook, 'we were just talking.'

'But you were fighting,' she insisted, her ears still ringing with the fearsome sounds of their exchange. They were more astonished. 'No, talking,' they insisted.

No one offended her so much by violence as Menaka in her carelessness. She watched disbelievingly as Menaka, telling her about a party she had been to, idly reached out her fingers and crumbled a sheaf of new buds on the small potted plant she had been labouring to grow on the balcony. 'Menaka!' she warned, on the edge of her chair, unable to bear the sight of such unthinking destruction any more.

'What?'

'You've broken all the buds!'

Menaka looked down in surprise. She had done it unconsciously, had not meant to destroy anything at all. Destruction came so naturally; that was the horror. Even the smallest, Karan, appeared to build a tower of blocks only for the pure, lustful joy of throwing it over with a great clatter, so much more enjoying the downfall than the architecture. She winced and shrank, hearing those blocks crash. The creative impulse had no chance, against the overpowering desire to destroy.

There had been the joy of finding Menaka, one Sunday morning, sitting at her work table with an array of paints and jars and brushes. She had hurried away so as not to disturb, having learnt how frailty the creative thread existed. Menaka occasionally painted. Guiltily, her mother, on a weekday when the girl was away at school, looked into her room and went through her water colours. A monsoon scene in which Menaka had used quantities of water to dilute the paints and give an authentic rendering of rain. Slabs of more solid paint to imply walls, bricks, and roofs. Insect legs, impersonating stems. Charmed, she carefully put them back. Saw them next in long tatters. She had heard that sound of ripping paper that made her stop, then run in, and found Menaka cross-legged on the bed, idly tearing her paintings to strips and dropping them on the floor. Taken aback by her mother's passionate, almost tearful reaction, Menaka said, 'But they're no good. They're not worth keeping.'

'They're not worth *destroying.*'

'If they're bad — why not?' Menaka shrugged. She was so slim, so perfectly made, her clear skin held her together so tautly and purely, her discipline and her instincts seemed inviolable. Yet she would casually crumble a sheaf of buds, rip up her paintings into shreds. Over this havoc, she viewed her mother with cool and candid eyes, and Sita, who had herself never been able to execute the simplest sketch and whose potted plants tended to go limp and rotten from too much watering, stared back in incomprehension.

'You frighten me,' Sita said and Menaka shrugged.

❧

'They frighten me — appal me,' she said, folding her arms about her, standing in the middle of the room when their guests had left.

Her husband looked at her with the family expression — cool, curious, uncomprehending. Their guests had been business associates of his; he had thought them pleasant, tolerable, although he had not given their characters much thought. People were, to him, friends, visitors, business associates, colleagues, or acquaintances. He regarded them with little humour and with restraint. With some he did business, with others he ate a meal. Some came to see him, others he visited. He found them very like himself and not worth much thought or introspection. Not an introvert, nor an extrovert — a middling kind of man, he was dedicated unconsciously to the middle way. So he could not tell what she meant or what she felt when she folded her arms about her and stared at the closed door, saying, 'They are *nothing* — nothing but appetite and sex. Only food, sex and money matter. Animals.'

'I thought you liked animals.'

'My pet animals — or wild animals in the forest, yes. But these are neither — they are like pariahs you see in the streets, hanging about drains and dustbins, waiting to pounce and kill and eat.'

He shook his head, baffled. The guests had been new acquaintances of his — a pair of brothers in business, large and jolly men with the sole gift of making money. One had brought a wife — a soft-fleshed, thick, jewel-embedded woman with nothing to say although her eyes roved over and scanned every detail of their room and seemed to absorb and put away details that she might later vociferously reveal. He had discussed his business with the men, ignored the woman and been neither bored nor exhilarated. It had been an ordinary evening. 'They are the Indian merchant class,' he said drily, 'to which I think we ourselves belong. Better get used to them.'

She never got used to anyone. When they lived, in the first years of their married lives, with his family in their age-rotted flat of Queens Road, she had vibrated and throbbed in revolt against their subhuman placidity, calmness, and sluggishness. The more stolid and still and calm they were, the more she thrummed, as though frantic with fear that their subhumanity might swamp her. She behaved provocatively — it was there that she started smoking, a thing that had never been done in their household by any woman and even by men only in secret — and began to speak in sudden rushes of emotion, as though flinging darts at the their smooth, unscarred faces.

The women half-smiled when she entered a room, and bent over their trays on which they were chopping vegetables — chopping, slicing, chopping, slicing the incredible quantities of vegetables they daily devoured. Like elephants, she thought — eating grass, shifting from foot to foot, swaying their trunks, small-eyed, eating. The whole house seemed to be a kitchen — kitchen smells filled each corner of it, everyone talked of the meal to come; if meals were not being eaten, then they were being cooked, or cleaned up after, or planned. Coming from the island where one had scarcely been aware of what one ate, where no one gave a moment's thought to food, and meals were hurried out of the way as quickly as possible.

Sita found this at first so fantastic as to be unreal. But very soon the kitchen odours and kitchen sounds thickened and swelled till they became indubitably real, overpoweringly real. She took to smoking instead of eating, to staring about her in silence, to speaking provocatively. They did not often answer her provocative questions, nor did they complain of her to her husband as women in another household might have done, for they had a quite exceptional capacity to expand the household and accept even such an outrageous outsider, and beyond that they did not stir themselves. They wished to be left in peace to eat, to digest. 'They're nothing, they're nothing,' she stormed in her room, when suffocated by their vegetarian complacence, the stolidity of the well-fed, and since she could not grow used to them as in the beginning he had hopefully urged her to do, and he had begun to suffer from appalling, inexplicable backaches, her husband sighed and moved to a small flat where they lived alone.

But living by themselves was little better. People continued to come and be unacceptable to her. She took their insularity and complacence as well as the aggression and violence of others as affronts upon her own living nerves. She spent almost all her time on the balcony, smoking, looking out at the sea. They had chosen this small flat because of the sea below it — the sea was to have come surging up and washed the city away, for her. Strangely enough, the sea carried very little away but brought much to those rocks on which it ceaselessly spilled, littering them with the rotten carcasses of fish, with stinking seaweed and with less explicable objects like a ring of green plastic, a rubber shoe, bones, and frayed tins. Throwing them up at her, the sea ran out, hissing, fold upon fold drawn back, drawn back till she shuddered to think what else it might reveal.

She sat there smoking, not even looking at the sea any more, till he exclaimed, 'Bored? How? Why? With what?' and could not begin to comprehend her boredom. She herself, looking on it, saw it stretched out so vast, so flat, so deep, that in fright she scrambled about it, searching for a few of these moments that proclaimed her still alive, not quite drowned and dead.

❧

Once, driving back from a week's holiday exploring the Ajanta and Ellora caves, along an immensely long and curiously empty road through a landscape of heaped rocks and grey-pillared banyan trees that looked like the petrified remains of some ancient vegetable civilization, Sita was woken out of her dishevelled sleep in the back seat where she lay in a tumble with the sleeping children, and found that her husband had stopped the car at the side of the road where an extraordinary looking, excessively blonde, tall, and stooped foreigner stood holding a large placard before his face with a kind of insane patience and hopefulness.

It was only after he had stopped that Raman saw the placard read *Ajanta.* 'I'm sorry, we've just come from Ajanta we're going the other way,' he apologized, for the lowering of the placard had revealed a sudden flowering of that near-albino face that made him feel apologetic. 'If you want a lift to Ajanta, you had better cross the road and stand on that side,' he advised him gently.

'Uh-oh;' the man smiled a small rabbit smile of self-deprecation. 'Yeah, I'd better,' he agreed, and shifted the pack on his shoulders as though it bruised him.

Raman seemed unusually moved and offered him a cigarette. Sita, sitting intently from the back seat, thanked him for his gentleness, thanked him ardently in silence, and leaned forward to take a cigarette herself. Raman lit both their cigarettes and they smoked nervously, Sita acutely conscious of this silent link between them of a shared physical act of inner nervousness. Smoking, the man leant in at the front window and began to talk with the easy confessional manner of his race. Within a few moments he had informed them that he used to play the flute in his college chamber orchestra, had won a scholarship to come to India and study the *shehnai,* had failed to get a degree here he shrugged, blinked but, rather than return to the West; had decided to wander about India 'for a bit'.

By the end of this story, he had come to the end of his cigarette, Sita of her's, and there seemed no reason, in this bleak, barely breathing plain, not to part. So he shifted his pack about his shoulders again, clinked, raised an arm in farewell and crossed over to the other side of the road looking, Sita thought, distressingly ineffectual, his paleness creating scarcely a mark, a blot, on that empty, heat-livid road. It seemed not even to cast a shadow.

Raman started the car, waved, shouted 'Good-bye, good luck,' and drove on.

She not only thought again and again of that wanderer's mirage like appearance and disappearance but spoke too often and too much of him. 'He seemed so brave,' she blurted out when Raman asked her why she had once more brought up the subject of the hitchhiking foreigner, months later.

'Brave? Him?' Raman was honestly amused. 'He was a fool — he didn't even know which side of the road to wait on.'

'Perhaps that was only innocence,' Sita faltered, 'and it made him seem more brave not knowing anything but going on nevertheless.'

He looked at her with astonishment, not having heard her praise fools before. On another occasion, when she had again spoken of him, he said, 'You seem to admire him a lot,' and there was annoyance in his voice. 'You would have liked to know him better, it seems.'

'I would,' she instantly agreed. 'I would like to travel like that myself,' and so plunged them into a state of tension that lasted till tension was no longer possible and died of itself. It was plain, during these mostly silent, occasionally snap and bark-interrupted days, that he regarded her admiration for and interest in the hitchhiker practically as an act of infidelity. She plainly agreed — although the boy had not attracted her physically, had repelled her by revealing, in those few moments, a number of physical habits that sickened her — his rapid blinking, his way of licking shreds of tobacco on his lips, of scratching his ear — but if her infidelity was only mental, it was so much more immeasurable for that and she still carried its deep scar.

Raman, as if in proud accusation, had never presented her with any similar grounds for suspecting him of even a mental act of infidelity. (She did not count the wistful look with which he spooned up these delicacies occasionally sent to him by an aunt or sister — she disdained them too much to pay them attention.) He hardly even complained of the backaches that wracked him.

When she looked at her wedding photographs, stiffly stuck into a large album that the children now and then dragged out and placed on her lap, insisting that she explain the curiosities inside that so amused them, she could scarcely recognize her bride self. She seemed to have adopted, for the occasion — the way an insect might adopt certain characteristics not of its own breed for the sake of camouflage and self-defence — the anonymous look of a shy, not wholly conscious bride, quite unlike her appearance at any other time. It was a look she had immediately discarded and lost. She was amused to turn from the album to the mirror and see the layers of experience and melancholy and boredom that had settled upon her face since then, like so much grey sand. She was not dismayed — on the contrary, she felt a kind of pride.

'Are you waiting for someone?' she was occasionally asked by one of the children dashing past or by her husband, as she sat out on the balcony, smoking, not reading the book on her lap, looking at and then away from the sea. Sometimes she answered with a nod for it was true, she was always waiting. Physically so resigned, she could not inwardly accept that this was all there was to life, that life would continue thus, inside this small, enclosed area, with these few characters churning around and then past her, leaving her always in this grey, dull-lit, empty shell. I'am waiting, she agreed — although for what, she could not tell: for the two halves of this grey egg-world to fall apart and burst into festival fireworks, a woman's seaweed hair or bloodstained feathers? For the revolution of the world to alter in one mighty swing that would fling them all, tiny grey sand-lice, into icy space? Somewhere such indiscretion, inspiration, and force. But, till she came to it, she would live on, smothered by this endlessly damp, soft grey sand, and it seemed that these years of her life were dyed, coloured through and through, with the colour of waiting. It was not a pure colour — it was tinged at times with anxiety, at others with resignation. Or with frenzy, patience, grimness, fears. But whatever its tint, its tone, it had seeped through her, flowed along every smallest capillary till she herself was turned to the colour of waiting, was turned a living monument to Waiting.

When there was the fifth baby to wait for, she rebelled. She would not wait for it to come, for anything to happen. She sank lower down into the cane basket chair and willed only that it would not be born and nothing would happen. It became unthinkable that anything should happen — for happenings were always violent. Karan kicked over a tower of blocks and howled with maniac glee to see them tumble; Menaka sat calmly tearing her Sunday watercolours into long strips of meaningless colour; her husband casually handed her the newspaper on his way out to office. They all hammered at her with cruel fists — the fallen blocks, the torn watercolours, the headlines about the war in Vietnam the photograph of a woman weeping over a small grave, another of a crowd outside a Rhodesian jail; articles about the perfidy of Pakistan, the virtuousness of our own India... They were hand-grenades all, hurled at her frail goldfish-bowl belly and instinctively she laid her hands over it, feeling the child there play like some soft-fleshed fish in a bowl of warm sea-water. She folded her hands over it, frightened, certain now that civilization had been created by the godlike efforts of the few, in the face of a constant, timeless war of destruction that had begun with time and was now roaring around her, battering her and her fish-foetus so that survival seemed hopeless. How could civilization survive, how could the child? How could she hold them whole and pure and unimpeached in the midst of this bloodshed? They would surely be wounded, fall and die.

Yet they continued and, with red and healthy blood in them, even flourished — the blocks were capable of rising in another structure, Menaka continued to grow more clear-skinned and soft-limbed and exquisite every minute, the newspapers were delivered regularly to her every day and, now and then, an actual shape, hard and alive, would push at the side of her belly an agitated, eager foot or fist. Holding her breath, she admitted that destruction may be the true element in which life survives; and creation merely a freak, temporary, and doomed event.

Then she grew muddled. By giving birth to the child now so safely contained, would she be performing an act of creation or, by releasing it in a violent, pain-wracked blood-bath, would she only be destroying what was, at the moment, safely contained and perfect? More and more she lost all feminine, all maternal belief in childbirth, all faith in it, and began to fear it as yet one more act of violence and murder in a world that had more of them in it than she could take.

'I won't have the baby,' she said, at first faintly, then defiantly.

'You're mad,' he said, simply.

The line between the creative and the destructive grew so thin, so hazy and undefinable that, gazing at it, she seemed to see it vanish altogether. But, instead, some lines she had read and remembered, wavered quite arbitrarily across her mind:

. . .even the slumbrous egg as it labours
under the shell
Patiently to divide and sub-divide. . . .

but could remember no more and was baffled.

It was Raman who first suggested escape to her. 'Where shall we go this summer?' he innocently asked, for every year he asked her that at that point in time when summer seemed to squat on its haunches, panting, unable to rise and move any further.

To Manori, she instantly replied, but in silence because with this idea there also sprang to her mind the idea that she would go alone. The plan to escape boiled up in her with such suddenness, she was herself taken by surprise, not realizing that it had been simmering inside her so long although she was herself the pot, the water and the fire.

Only after he had decided that he could not get away that summer after all — the labourers at the factory were threatening to go on strike — she told him her plan, safe now from pursuit and capture. 'I shall go to Manori,' she said.

The island had been buried beneath her consciousness deliberately, for years. Its black magic, its subtle glamour had grown too huge, had engulfed her at a time when she was still very young and quite alone. She had grown afraid of it, been relieved to leave it and come to the mainland with Raman. The mainland — the very word implied solidity, security: the solidity of streets, the security of houses. She had not realized then that living there would teach her only that life was a crust of dull tedium, of hopeless disappointment — but a thin crust, a flimsy crust that, at every second or third step, broke apart so that she tumbled in, with the most awful sensation, into a crashed pile of debris. She had no longer the nerve or the optimism to continue. No, she refused to walk another step. She would turn, go back and find the island once more.

part two

winter '47

They had been blown towards the island, that first time, on the waves of a silk-smooth sea, rippling with enthusiasm, bounding with anticipation, sparkling with hope. The boat skimmed towards the island not only on account of the pleasant west coast winter breeze but on account of an airy atmosphere created by her father's graceful, expressive gestures as he waved to those of his followers who had had to stay back on the mainland, weeping, and then turned to those *chelas* who were coming with him and his family, bundled together in the boat like children on a picnic, laughing. With those same gentle, rounded movements, he lifted the malodorous garlands of rose and marigold off his neck and handed some to his children, some to his *chelas.* The children draped them about their own necks, the *chelas* flung them far into sea and laughed to see them bob on the waves like coloured ducks. He smiled, he smoothened the silver wisps of hair across the majestic mahagony dome of his head. The streamers of the boat blew in the wind. The boat landed. The passengers bounded out. He followed. It was an auspicious landing.

Seeing the bullock cart, freshly painted and festooned with crackling white and pink streamers, Sita gave a jump. Her brother, younger but more contained, smiled with sly satisfaction, immediately looking away as though he did not really care. Their father placed his arm — lightly, momentarily — on their elder sister's shoulder, as if urging her to see and approve. The *chelas* helped them into the gay cart — they were going to follow on foot, they shouted, almost sang, carrying bits of luggage on their backs — and they flew on.

Down the dusty road between the pink fluttering sheets of Bombay duck hung out to dry in the crisp sun, up the grassy knoll to the house that had been gifted to them by a Parsi millionaire, Dalwala, the richest and most recent of their father's admirers. 'It is a small return for the great difference you have made in my life,' he had said, slightly bowing as he stood beside the father who reclined on a straw mat, still weak after an incredibly long fast in the cause of freedom. 'Only a token of my respect,' he had said, and then stood aside so that his servants could place a tray of pomegranates, sweet limes, and bananas on the floor beside the mat. Lolling weakly on a white bolster, father had faintly smiled. 'I always wanted,' he confessed, 'to find a village where I could put my social theories into practice. I have been theorizing for too many years. I should like to experiment now. Manori will be perfect.' Mr. Dalwala had humbly bowed his head, his face utterly serious. Father was smiling.

As they rolled under the coconut palms — ducking their heads, the bullocks had rushed into the shade with such helter-skelter eagerness — they saw the new house, as white as a washed shell, on top of the knell, and its name freshly painted on a signboard beside a hibiscus bush in full bloom: *Fiona.* (Mr. Dalwala had studied, strange to say, in Scotland, at St Andrew's.) Sita thought it beautiful. But her father, smiling his most puckish smile, waved away that incongruous name. 'I shall call it *Jeevan Ashram,'* he declared, 'the Home of the Soul.' Thus he would transform the house, thus the whole island.

From the open veranda, wind-swept and pillared, two strangers came down to greet the family — a perspiring, purple young man in a *lungi* of green checked cotton, who told them he was Moses and a woman, round-thighed, yellow-eyed, encased in a pink skirt and an orange blouse like some ripe fruit, at whom he pointed, saying, 'Miriam, my wife.' Father beamed. 'Moses and Miriam,' he repeated, 'the original inhabitants of our paradise,' and seemed pleased with this particular incongruity.

The children dodged around those two stalwart bodies and raced up the stairs to the veranda, then through the house, from room to room, and found an open outdoor staircase that led to a large room on top in which they were at one level with the palm tree tops. Leaning out of the windows, trying to grab at the coconuts, they saw the *chelas* coming slowly up the road, a little more silent, more tired than when they had left them at the landing-place. They waved, the *chelas* smiled and shouted and came along faster.

'Fiona?' they shouted, stopping at the signboard. 'Fiona!' they hooted.

'No, *Jeevan Ashram,'* said father, standing at the top of the veranda stairs from where he could see, beyond the grove of palms and casuarinas, the silky morning sea.

Mr. Dalwala had bought the plot on the island and built the house, named it *Fiona* and piled its verandas with striped beach cushions, then proudly brought his bride to it, only to discover that she hated the old fashioned bungalow, hated the rough island and declared that if he must have a house for weekend parties, she would take a smarter shack on a nearer beach, Juhu. Mr. Dalwala could have sold it to one of the British commercial firms in Bombay that kept weekend shacks for their higher-scale employees, but in 1947 the fate of the British firms was somewhat uncertain and not one wished, precisely at that point in history, to indulge in luxuries. Mr. Dalwala was already acquainted with father, had heard him speak at crowded assemblies in the city and found him the most overpowering personality he had met, so when he heard, just at that time, that father intended to retire from politics — 'My goal is achieved,' he had said when India's independence was declared, in a voice so weak from fasting that the words seemed humble and self-effacing, not proud or triumphant — he offered him, with that old-fashioned humility and courtesy, the stranded sea-shell, *Fiona.* 'A place for you to rest and recuperate,' he had suggested, 'a small return for the great difference... a token of my respect. ...' Father, smiling, accepted. 'Manori will be perfect,' he said, and chose a pomegranate from the tray of fruits.

Sita came hurtling down to join her father on the veranda and greet the *chelas* as they straggled up, laughing at the dust that coloured them grey. 'There are green coconuts on the trees,' she called to them. 'Did you see the *cheekoos* on the trees there — small brown ones? And Jeevan has seen a pond — he's gone to see if there are frogs. Father, look, you can see the sea from here!'

He smiled at her. 'Of course,' he said, 'we're on an island,' and the sea lay sparkling and the air reflected it. Flashes of light skidded, bubbles of light rose and floated. There was an effervescence in the air that made Sita kick up her heels and prance like a pony. She was not really a child at that time — in another environment she might have already been regarded as a young woman, but she had lived a strange life, an unusual life, that had the effect of making her withdraw into the protective chrysalis of childhood for longer than is usual for most. She saw the island as a piece of magic, a magic mirror — it was so bright, so brilliant to her eyes after the tensions and shadows of her childhood. It took her some time to notice that this magic, too, cast shadows.

❧

The very gaiety and laughter and animation of that winter seemed magic and unreal because it was in such startling contrast to the life they had lived so far — this family with its father and its band of disciples. As far as Sita could tell from her own experience, their lives had been lived inside jails, in crowded assemblies, in mobs, in slums, tenements, and villages where life was not picturesque or calm, but harsh and barbaric. They had known all the tensions of political life, although only on the brink of it, and its cruelties. There had been long separations, dark seclusions. There had been austerity and fear. It was always made clear to Sita that this was no age for games or sweets but one for prayer and sacrifice. Having no true alternative, she accepted it.

Now she saw it flung to the winds, to the sea, like a cloud that disintegrates and disappears, leaving each wave on the sea to sparkle like a piece of mica. The *chelas* played games of *kho* in the casuarina grove and filled the house with their emotional singing — possibly they, too, were recovering their lost childhood. There were visitors from the mainland. There were plans, programmes, meetings — and then, with joyful disobedience, these would be forgotten and all would pour out on to the terrace and sit about chatting instead, or race each other down to the beach for a swim. Youth seemed to have come upon them newly — having passed through such bitter maturity already, they met it with greater abandon.

No one, neither these suddenly childish, exuberant *chelas,* nor the villagers who were attracted to the house by its buoyant new life and came, ostensibly with gifts of fish or coconuts, and actually to satisfy their curiosity, seemed to realize that it was all a creation, a construction of the father's that they were a part of an experiment he was making. Not that he did not tell them this — he told them very often, at meetings and discussions, and made it all very clear to them, and very pleasant. Yet no one could decide — the fact that all his biographers avoided this issue proved this — the precise nature of this experiment. Had it been religious? Or social? Or moral? No one ever defined it. Religious, possibly.

He prayed, it was true, a great deal. He told them, jocularly, 'I never had time for it before independence. There was too much practical work to be done. Now I am an old man, I have arrived at the age for preparing to meet my maker,' and he pointed to that long, bare room upstairs and said, 'That will be my prayer-room.' He had led them up the outdoor staircase to it, stood by its window and appeared pleased. It was a pleasing room — in its white-washed, bare length and with its many windows that let in the sharp white light of the winter sky and made it seem almost a part of the grove — coconut, casuarina, and *cheekoos* — that surrounded it. Beyond it the beach and the sea glittered and dazzled. He had unrolled his straw mat in the centre of the stone floor and there he prayed — several times a day, at such length that for a time they were awed, his family and his *chelas,* and kept at a distance and tried to be quiet during his prayer hours.

Very soon, however, those private prayers extended to include the devotions of all his *chelas,* not only under pressure of their love for him and their need to be close to him but because he himself, having lived most of his years in the midst of pressing crowds, seemed no longer to mind their numbers or their noise. Then not one but many lamps were lit, and a Bengali *chela* took to summoning them for prayers with an enormous conch shell that made them laugh with its grotesque, bursting groans and yet brought them surging up the stairs as though to a party. The elder daughter's *tanpura* was placed on a mat at one end of the room and, twice a day, there would swell and roll the poignant devotional music of a great temple. It would begin with a few notes, or even verses, sung in the exquisite voice of the elder daughter (she who became India's leading devotional singer, began her career in that white room on the island) and then the *chelas* would join in, singing the refrain, clapping in time, so that the music rolled and rose with a power to rival the nearby sea's.

In their midst the father would sit immobile, his eyes closed, the palms of his hands upturned on his knees, praying. Eventually those community devotions, with their festival atmosphere and sounds, seemed to grow too vociferous for him and, although he attended them and smiled with them and swayed in time to the music quite properly, he took to praying outside. He would rise to his feet just as the room began to vibrate with the impassioned sound of their singing, led by Rekha's piercing tones, and descend alone to the terrace where Sita and Jivan sat playing.

Sometimes he sat down on one of the stone seats along the balustrade, his face raised to the sky, his eyes closed and such an expression of intensity on his face that the children preferred to slip quietly away into the foliage of the *cheekoo* trees. Or he would go down the steps into the grove and there pace up and down, his hands folded behind his back, his eyes half-shut. Sita would wake at dawn to the sound of the *tanpura* and Rekha's trilling song, and roll out into the morning light which had a mother-of-pearl tenderness to it at that hour, and see his massive figure, clothed in marmoreal white, gravely pacing the casuarina needle-spread earth of the grove below their house. Kneeling sleepily on the stone bench, she would watch him — how his head and shoulders beneath the low boughs, descend by a flight of broken stairs to the beach and there his slowly-pacing, statuesque figure would resemble one of those white water birds that marked the sands with their starred footprints. The fisherfolk on the beach stopped to watch him pass. Soon they began to call greetings to him, respectfully. He looked very much a saint.

Social, too, one could call that island experiment.

'No water? No well?' he had asked incredulously, on first entering the house. 'We must make one,' he decided.

'Yes, yes — I will see to it — a tubewell, costing perhaps — umm,' began Mr. Dalwala in embarrassed haste, but father cut him short quite brusquely, saying, 'No, I will have no machines here. I can prove that machinery is not essential to civilization, even that it is inimical. For Indian civilization, I think it is fatal. Gandhi taught us that.'

'But then — ?'

'We shall dig,' father said, spreading out his hands to show how long and strong his fingers were, how supple his wrists. They were the hands of a peasant. He called for a spade and walked down the knoll to the coconut grove by Moses' hut. 'Here,' he said, bending over and digging out the first spadeful. With cries, laughing like children shown a new game, his *chelas* leapt forward and knelt on the ground and began to dig with their hands, or chips of stone, or sticks. But after a while they fell back and Sita was not surprised to see how shallow the hollow was, barely a scratching of the surface. Mr. Dalwala also frowned worriedly and began to murmur about tubewells under his breath. But father said, his voice booming out with sudden force that recalled the speeches he had made as a young revolutionary, 'We shall dig for two hours every morning and two hours every evening, after prayers.' Mr. Dalwala sighed and said he would send them spades.

The well was dug — no more a miracle, perhaps, than the wells in any village, but somehow it seemed one. The very presence of the father, watching and directing his *chelas,* all in white, all still pure and clear as glass after their prayers and devotions, made it seem one. Its sides were paved with stones. Pulleys were attached to strong posts and buckets let down. The first bucketful was drawn out and father ladled out the water to each of those who had helped with the digging.

'Sweet!' they cried, ecstatic, as they cupped their hands beneath the ladle and drew in mouthfuls of water. 'Sweet!'

Sita also came forward and her father, after hesitating for a second, smiled and filled her cupped hand from the ladle. She drank and pulled a face, understanding in an instant his hesitation, for it was not sweet. But she was either too loyal or too disappointed to say so in front of that large, waiting circle of *chelas* and villagers. Only later, down on the beach with her brother, she confessed to its awful taste — and felt contrite, all night, for her betrayal, her failure to find the well water sweet.

And under what heading could one place his unorthodox ministrations to the village folk? Not exactly medical. They had so fantastic an element in them. Yet he had not himself initiated what his *chelas* later called, some in awe and some in puzzlement, his 'miracle cures'. They were initiated by a fisherwoman who claimed, after daily drinking water from the well, to be cured of her boils. She brought two moss-covered crabs in a basket one day and flung herself at his feet and touched the ground before them with her forehead. 'The well is blessed,' she declared, 'my boils are gone.' Father stepped back and seemed thrown off his balance for a moment, till he understood and accepted this element in his career, and he smiled, saying nothing. Sita was too happy with the crabs, tilting the basket this way and that to see them put out their claws and cling to its weave, to take special notice either of his smile or his silence. But she did remember this woman, Champa of the pocked face, to be the first of what turned into a procession that came up from the village, through the grove, to father's 'clinic'.

Then strange things happened, one after the other, with rapidity.

The beautiful fisherwoman, Phoolmaya, who had been married to the fisherman Raju for ten years and been childless and was almost taunted to suicide by her mother-in-law, came up the steps to weep at father's feet when he sat praying on the veranda. It was very early in the morning; the fishing fleet that had set out before dawn could still be seen, riding on the billowing line of the horizon, pulled along swiftly as by a giant with a string, and the gulls were like twinkles, sparkles flung up into the opal sky. Father seemed not to listen to her, but gazed out at the boats as they sped along the horizon, their white sails withdrawing one by one till they vanished. Then he looked down at her as she crouched, still weeping and striking her head with her braceleted arm, and said 'Yes', and then asked her courteously to come up to the room upstairs to pray with him. Soon after Phoolmaya came bearing vessels of oil, red hibiscus, and green coconuts, her husband trailing behind her, trying not to look foolish, for Phoolmaya was pregnant. She had a son. She lost her beauty and her poignancy, she began to look coarse and the wear and tear to show, but she had her son.

There was old Kanti-amma who came at a run, screaming through long, hanging driblets of spittle, 'My child has been bitten! Babaji! Babaji!' She rolled on the floor, her eyes dilated and starting out from her skull, tearing her hair till father, who was then eating his single meal of the day, came out to see her. Then he moved with speed. He hurried with her to the village where she kept pigs in a drain that ran around her hut. Stepping over the drain, he went into the hut. The child had been bitten by one of the scorpions that infested the rotten thatch of the hut and occasionally dropped to the floor. Father had brought medicines in the pocket of his *kurta* and he drew them out, sprinkled on something dark that glittered and something in sharp crystals that shone, and the poison began to bubble and froth and something oozed out and dribbled down the child's foot. He wailed louder at the sight of the poison but the people who stood in the doorway, crowding in, heavily breathing as they stared, shouted, 'Look, the poison has run out!'

'Hot fomentations,' father said in the stypic tones of a doctor, and showed Kanti-amma how to apply them before he went back to the house, holding Sita by one hand and Jivan by the other.

What was quite the strangest part of it, Kanti-amma for years told anyone willing to listen, was that no more scorpions dropped to the floor or bit anyone again. 'He did magic,' she hissed, her eyes popping so that small children were frightened by her and said, 'She's mad,' but 'He knew magic,' she screeched after them, so that they fell over her pigs as they ran.

Kanti-amma first used the word 'magic', not father. The villagers repeated it, not the *chelas.* Who, then, began the legend? He was the legend but whether he began it by plan and deliberation, or acquired it by force of pressure from the simple people around him, remained a matter for debate.

They came to the well, morning and evening, with their buckets, a line of women with their round vessels upon their hips and, as they waited for their turn at the well, it was natural they should speak of the man who had dug it. Sita and Jivan liked to play in the clay and slush around it and so they heard the legend when it was still being composed. It was not, at that time, a fluent and accurate composition — no, it was full of stops and starts and alterations, continually bringing them into corners of darkness again.

'So Babaji lifted the lantern — high, above his head — and stared — and in the lamp-light we could all see the cobra,' an old woman declaimed, hoarsely, displaying a fine feeling for the theatre in her sudden gestures and her contorted expressions. 'It had a black hood and its eyes glittered — like jewels. It was ready to strike. But Babaji stood with the lantern — steady, steady, not shaking — and with one hand he pushed back my husband who wanted to kill it with a rock, the fool — and then the cobra bowed — like *this* — and slipped *backwards* into its hole. And Mata began to scream that we should not let it go or it would come back and kill us in the night, but Babaji — he looked like this — and he said, "No, Mata, it will never come again." *Did* it come?' she harangued them through her ochre teeth.

'Babaji says we must not kill.'

'What, not even snakes or scorpions? Are we to be killed instead?' some young and scornful voice cried, making two pails clank together loudly.

'All is holy, he says.'

'Even killers?'

'Ah, Babaji does magic so they *cannot* kill,' the old ochre-toothed woman triumphed. She put her two fists beneath her chin and tossed her head at the girl, defiantly. 'He knows magic for taking death out of all creatures.'

Sita and Jivan, physically quite placid as they slapped cakes of mud flat on the sand, exchanged deep looks, thinking of the games they played on the beach together. Today they had buried a live frog they had found, in a deep grave in the sand; beneath a rock they had decorated with palms, fronds and hibiscus blooms. Then, guiltily, they had come away, solemn with the secret death of the frog.

'Do you think,' Sita whispered, 'he can take death out of *us?*' and Jivan glared at her coldly as though he did not know what she meant. He played their games with greater ardour and dedication than she did but, unlike her, insisted on keeping them locked in a secret compartment of his chameleon existence. He watched this village theatre by the well intently but never discussed it.

'Not magic,' the young woman grumbled, 'he has medicines, that's all. Medicines for everything. Don't you see him take them out of his pocket? He has some even for the soil. He was speaking to my man about it when we were in the fields, planting brinjals. He told us the name of the medicine we must put in the soil to make brinjals grow. Medicines for the soil!' She threw back her head and laughed artificially.

'It is right,' another claimed indignantly. 'Don't we put fish manure around the roots of the coconut palms? Don't you know anything? Born empty, weren't you? Eh?' She looked around at the other woman, exhorting them to laugh, and they laughed.

The children were a bit disappointed — the notes were jumbled, the whole bar had foundered — but it was true that this magical, fantastical element of their father's career had a daylight, practical aspect, too. That was what baffled his *chelas,* his biographer and his critics and made them hold their tongues. Practical achievements and shady hocus-pocus wound in and out of each other to form one inextricable strand, knotted but whole.

All remembered how he walked barefoot in the muddy, ploughed fields down by the village where the islanders grew some meagre crops of vegetables and rice. He bent double with them deep in the mud, showing them how to space the rice seedlings. 'Try my method,' he coaxed. 'Just see if this crop won't be different from your last.' It would have been — all saw the grain packing the pale sheaths, white and full — had some unforeseen, unexpected pest not blighted that beautifully planted crop.

He had not the time to plant a second crop. It was all unfortunate but at least a few of them remembered how, before the pest appeared and ruined it all, the rice had looked that year in its ripe-green promise. They loved him, recalling it. They remembered how he had carried a bucket down from the big white house to the well for water in the morning, before anyone of his household was stirring. Some ran forward to seize the bucket from his hand and others — who had been to the mainland and knew of such things — said. 'Why not lay pipes to the house, Babaji? Then you could get water straight from taps.' To both he shook his head, saying, 'No, I have come to live on the island like an islander. I will fetch my water from the well like you,' and walked on, barefoot, bareheaded, dressed in homespun, carrying loads like them.

His *chelas* called him a saint, his critics a charlatan, the villagers a wizard, and each produced evidence to prove his theory. All evidence could be verified, but it led the student in no one direction and all that could be said, as Sita said in her maturity, was that he had begun his life 'in service' and then realized — she remembered that moment of realization, that faint smile when the pock-marked, hysterical Champa had touched his feet with her forehead — that self-sacrifice and service place power in a man's hand, ennoble and enlarge a human being into a super human being (especially in a setting of ignorance and poverty and gullibility) and how, once this super-humanity is recognized (that procession coming up through the coconut grove with offerings of oil and hibiscus and fish) it can be used as a means to power and glory, not of a cause (a cause is abstract, unattractive to the poor and ignorant) but of one's own self — solid, primary and obvious as an idol in the temple of the simple. He had fought, whole-heartedly and earnestly, for a cause, and won. What could he go on to doing then? He himself became a cause, and won again. Won. The island belonged to him.

❧

On this island, strange experiences and strange sensations made her think and grow too large for the chrysalis of children and so she slowly, unwillingly emerged. She felt this strangeness in the atmosphere not altogether comfortable, as a moth that has emerged from its cocoon not into sunlight, but into a grey nonlight that does not warm the damp wings or give them strength for flight.

The first, the very first prickle down the spine that told her that her father's daylight, practical charisma had its underlit night-time aspect, was perhaps not such an extraordinary and after all, although its cause may — or may not — have been unconventional. Observing that it was always across the older sister's stolid shoulders that he placed his arm when they descended from the terrace to the casuarina grove and strolled out across the beach to watch the sun melt into the sea and the *chelas* pelt each other with sand-pies, observing how it was always her guarded eyes he met during a moving passage in the morning's devotional songs, observing how he stretched out his hand and squeezed her fingers when thay sat on the veranda and watched some young *chela's* pranks and charades — perhaps it was no unusual prick of jealousy that chilled Sita.

She went on to observe, coldly, how different this eldest sister was from her and her young brother. Neither of *them,* the proud young Sita maintained, had that dragging jaw, those thickly round shoulders, those weighted, drooping eyelids. Yes, they were untidy, ragged and wild, she knew, but that was because she and Jivan were quick and sprang and danced on the veranda, flew down from the wall into a bed of casuarina needles and raced on the dunes to send the terns screaming into the air.

Rekha, on the other hand, never appeared to move at all; she sat cross-legged and her thighs rose like two cushions before her and on them she placed her short, stubby hands that she moved, mechanically and gracelessly, in time to the music. Sita had to admit that Rekha, unlike her and Jivan, had a gift — she could sing. Day and night she was reminded of this one glory her sister possessed. It was what she heard at daybreak — her sister's voice spinning out the silken thread of a morning *raga* in that quiet hour before the *chelas* had risen for prayers.

When Sita rolled out of her bed and went out on the veranda in her short slip, her hair in a murky tumble, her eyes still blue with sleep, to see the white sea birds sparkle in the pastel sky and the fishing fleet already out on the mauve line of the horizon, a procession of brave white triangles riding the wind still sharp with the chill of the night, she heard Rekha, in the attic that was the prayer room, singing as if she were the bird that heralded the day. She could picture to herself her father's face as he leant against a bolster and shut his eyes in ecstasy, sipping in the finely distilled wine of that pure voice. She knew how he would half-open his eyes and watch Rekha's fingers as they ran over and over the three strings of her *tanpura* and her face, square and expressionless, immobile but for the lips that parted to let out the voice in one unsullied stream.

There seemed to be no relationship at all between that heavy, brooding body and the voice that greeted the sun like some goddess's, like some inhuman, unsubstantial creature's, and finally woke the *chelas* so that they came stumping up the stairs to sway and sing and clap to the music till they were in a state near that of dervishes; that later rang out on All India Radio every morning, all over the country, singing the first pure *bhajan* of the day. But her father, she saw, seemed to see the relationship between the two quite clearly for it was always the big girl's heavy shoulders that he fondled, her face that he scanned as she sat singing across the room from him.

Brooding over this disparity between them, Sita chose to voice it with a false lack of pride. 'Why can't you and I sing, Jivan, when she sings *so* well?'

That was out on the beach where they sat on their heels, watching a well they had dug slowly fill with clear water.

'Sisters should be a *little* alike,' Sita added since Jivan merely sat there with his arms clasped about his knees, watching.

'But you are not sisters,' he said then.

'Well, we are really — even if we don't look it.' Here Sita became her proud self with the long neck and the brilliant eyes.

'*Who* says so?' he said with scorn digging his toes in so that the silver rim of the well crumbled into the pool. 'She is only your step-sister.'

'*Who* says so?' cried Sita, leaping up and sending one whole side of the wall crashing with the pressure of her agitated foot. 'That is one of your stories, Jivan,' for Jivan was famous, notorious, for his 'stories.'

'It is not,' he said, getting up now that the well was spoilt. 'Ask father.'

Of course she could not. Throughout their stay on the island, she could not verify Jivan's story. But his words had dropped on her skin like acid and she felt them burn whenever she caught an exchange of that heavy-lidded look between father and daughter, or his arm in its fine white sleeve lie fondlingly across her round shoulders. It was true she admitted, that Rekha did resemble their father more than she or Jivan did. 'But that is because *we* take after *our* mother,' Jivan told her, Sita could not contradict, having no recollection of that dim relation. 'Your stories,' she scoffed sadly.

It was one more relationship that had to remain shrouded, a ghost in her life, because of the impossibility of talk between her and her father. There he was — so gentle, thoughtful, barefoot, dressed in homespun, fetching water from the well, a figure she respected, admired, and adored, was told by all to respect, admire, and adore — yet she could not talk to him. Perhaps because she never found him alone — always with Rekha silent at his side, or in the centre of a ring of young, fanatic, brillant-eyed *chelas* who also wore homespun, walked barefoot, and respected, admired, and adored him. She told herself she could never approach him to ask of such private and, somehow, secret matters. As an adult, later, she asked herself, had there been *no* opportunity ever of talking alone to him? Ah. She remembered, with an instinctive shrinking from the shock and the pain, a few strange moments, still unexplained. How he had sent her to fetch a lantern from Moses' hut and then come down the path, under the palms, to meet her half-way as she returned with it, hurrying because of the stories Miriam had told her of bleeding ghosts with twisted feet and the sound of the dry palm leaves clattering, clashing together — suddenly, precipitately — in the salt wind. They had not talked. He had met her with the sweetest chuckle and reached out his hand to chuck her chin. The hiss of the spurting wind, the rattle of those harsh leaves, had made her brush away his hand and rush up to the house, the lantern hysterically swinging. Why? There had been other occasions — a few... but she shrank away from them, shutting them away in the dark. They had all been wordless and agitated by the queerest, the most horrible sensations. Only once she had come close, very close, to asking.

It was a night when she had woken up, as she not infrequently did, disturbed by the light and the talk in the attic above that never seemed to be quiet or empty. She found herself so wide awake — having fallen asleep at an unaccustomedly early hour that evening — that she could not remain still in bed and went out, then strolled up the stone staircase with some vague thought of laying down on a mat in the attic and letting the *chelas* there entertain her in the pleasant light of the lanterns. But she saw through the open doorway that she had been mistaken — there was no gathering there tonight but only her father and an old friend of his who had come from the mainland to visit them for a few days.

Her father was seated at a low desk, his heavy, round shoulders bent about his work almost in a semicircle. The lantern was placed precariously on the edge of the desk, lighting its surface and the objects on it exclusively. She saw that his large peasant's hands were balled up and were rolling, mashing, rolling, mashing some gritty objects in a tiny pestle and mortar. She had seen him at this work before — ever since he had given in to the frenzied appeals of the villagers for medicines and begun to crush herbs, roots, pills and powders together in that small black mortar and then to divide them into the little paper packets that he kept in a bag and distributed amongst the villagers of whom hardly one was not afflicted in some hideous way or the other.

But tonight there was no sound of rustling leaves or pulpy roots being mashed or ground. Nor was there any odour of crushed berries or herbs. There was a far sharper sound, as of glass being ground, and no odour. Coming to stand, silently, in the doorway, she could look down on the top of that low desk in its circle of light, and she saw a small glass dish filled with small pellets of coloured and glass-like objects. She understood now why they made that sharp, breaking sound for they were jewels. She stood swaying in the dark with doubt and fear of hallucination, and heard father's friend, a dear friend, old and bumbly and bearded, say with incredulity, 'You *can't* believe in it yourself, Baba. You studied chemistry at school with me! Don't tell me you believe pearls and gold have therapeutic value?'

'No,' came the soft, bubbling reply, made effervescent with something like laughter. 'No student of chemistry can believe that. Anyone who has seen as much of life as I have, can't believe that. But what have these islanders seen? Nothing. Where have they ever been? Nowhere. *Their* faith has never been shaken. And do you deny the therapeutic value of faith? They believe gold is the best thing on earth — best because most valuable. So why not add a little to these powders with which I treat their boils and tumours? They believe it does them good and then it really does.'

'What about possible *harm?*' the old man was rigid, his arm stretched out as if in protest against the fraud, the danger.

Father soothed him. 'No, no, no,' he bubbled a laughing reply. 'Such minute quantities, Deedar, as I can afford, are just enough to make the powders sparkle and make the poor fellows see that I am really doing my best for them, more than any doctor would.'

Sita sank slowly back, step by step into the darkness, not caring to see or hear more. Twilight, shade and silence — these made up not only the natural but the necessary atmosphere of the island. She went back to her pallet and lay looking out of the open door at the indigo darkness that the sharp shapes of bats' wings now and then cut and sliced and at the palm trees turned to monuments of blackened silver by the moonlight.

She could talk, it seemed, only out on the beach where the sea and the sky were brilliantly lit and open to each other and her brother Jivan was totally unperturbed by anything that happened. His imperturbability was reassuring, so she told him.

'Gold and pearls, Jivan, rubies and diamonds! He just crushes them up — like sand. *Where* does he get them from? I thought we were *poor.* We're *supposed* to be poor.' She wore a frock that was ragged and patched. She owned no shoes. All she had that remotely resembled a jewel, an ornament, was a shell she had found the size and colour of an infant's ear that she prized and kept in an empty cigarette packet. Yet her father sat crushing pearls to pieces, mercilessly laughing — for some reason, laughing.

'They're mother's jewels, I suppose. She must have left them with him.'

'When she died?'

Jivan turned over a rock to see if there were a crab beneath it. 'Died?' he murmured. 'She didn't die — she ran away, to Benares.'

'Ran away? And left us?' Sita stood clutching her hair about her ears and feet sinking rapidly into the sand. Then she shook her head and let her hair all come loose and stamped her foot so that one footprint in the silver sand was deeper than all the others, one desperate footprint among the oblivious others. 'Your stories, Jivan,' she shouted. 'What stories you tell!'

'I'm telling you,' he agreed in that same flat tone that she had never heard altered (of course she had not seen him now for nearly twenty years, only read of him in the more disreputable papers that specialize in revealing shady secrets of notorious politicians, and she avoided them nowadays). 'You needn't believe me if you don't want to. But I've heard people talk about it. Of course,' he added, hurling down a rock upon a crab that tried to escape, 'she may be dead by *now.*'

Sita preferred to accept that. A mother alive and well in a place no further than Benares would have been an idea she could not cope with, used to being without one. Life seemed complete, full, without her, there was no reason for her to exist. Sita had imagined she came into the world motherless — and the world was crowded enough so. She had always lived in the centre of a crowd, having been one of those flower children of the independence movement whose chins were chucked by chuckling freedom fighters in homespun, who had spent hours at a stretch, mosquito-bitten legs dangling, at the edge of the dais on which politicians-in-waiting sat cross-legged before lowered microphones, addressing vast crowds beneath them. One sees them in old photographs, printed now in anniversary numbers of political magazines

— these wan, moth-eyed children, reflectively regarding the white-and-black masses below them as they sit on the raised dais, with, the leaders.

With calm eyes she had watched the surge and flow of such masses, listened to endless speeches on one subject, *Swaraj,* had her chin chucked, collected discarded garlands and played with the tinsel till she fell asleep against a bolster and was carried away to someone's house to sleep — always a different someone, it scarcely mattered which one. She belonged, if to anyone, to this whole society that existed at that particular point in history — like a lamb does to its flock — and saw no reason why she should belong to one family alone. As she was not sent to school, she only came in contact with other families like her own and life seemed normal. She could not remember wanting or waiting for her mother. The rubies and pearls crushed in the mortar were all she had seen of her.

The rubies and pearls shocked her. In that always murmuring casuarina grove, that always animated house on the knoll with its meetings, its gathers, its music, its shift and flow of ideas and activities, she now felt herself separated from them, the chosen one, chosen by the ghost for a flashing vision of its jewels although it remained invisible and fleshless itself. Sita found herself turning into a wanderer, always in search of the ghost. Who, what was she?

Women in Benares wore white and had shaven heads. With brass vessels in their shrivelled hands, they stumbled, half-fell down the cracked stone stairs to the river at dawn and squatted up and down its flotsam-edged banks, muttering their prayers. What prayers did her mother pray — the ritual prayers to Dawn, to the Sun, to the Ganges, or personal prayers of accusation, bitterness and reproach? Then, as the steps grew more crowded and the river filled with the bobbing beads of the bathers, and as she heaved herself out, her soaked white widow's garments clinging to her shanks, where did she go with her *lota* filled with Ganges water? Up the stairs, down the narrow alley still blackened with night as with kohl, edging past a white bull that calmly chewed the garlands offered to the many altars of the city, hurrying up another, narrower flight of stairs through which the fine roots of a banyan tree silently insinuated themselves, through the arched doorway of an old, rimed house — whose house? What room? And why?

'Rekha would know,' Jivan said when questioned. 'She's older than us — she will remember:'

'But we can't ask *her.*'

'*Ask* her,' he laughed with sudden wickedness, the pink gums above his broad teeth showing in the sudden bared obscenity of such loaded laughter. 'Let's see what she says!'

Sita's thin shoulders twitched in refusal — there was no intimacy between her and Rekha that would permit such a question.

Why had she left? She continued to wonder. Why had she left three children — Rekha, who, it was true, may not have been her own but another woman's child, the child of another ghost in her father's life; Jivan, the quick, clever, unscrupulous and irresistible boy, and Sita? Why had she left her husband whom they called the Second Gandhi? Why was she not at the island with them, participating in this experiment that all called unique, great, and Gandhian? Did she not agree with them?

It was a fevered time, this haunted time, but, like fever, it naturally ebbed and other matters heaved out of the surrounding sea and buried it, washed it away, leaving the barest residue of curiosity in Sita.

Later, after her marriage, her husband tried, for her sake, to locate this ghost in white, stripped of its jewels, lost in Benares. But no trace was found. All efforts, all enquiries drew a blank. Benares was flooded with the lost, the runaway, the dying and the dead of Hindu society. There they burned upon the pyres, danced about the pyres, fed the pyre with fuel, oil, and their own flesh, performing the dance of Shiva with their bodies, their limbs, their lives and souls. She was, or had been, one of them — that was all they knew of her. Sita shrugged when her husband returned from Benares and gave up the pursuit. 'After all, I can't put her photograph in the papers, can I?' she mused, 'I don't have one,' and let it go at that. But she wondered, at times, if it was because of what she had seen that night that had made her, years later, marry that very Deedar's son.

Only connect, they say. So she had spent twenty years connecting, link by link, this chain. And what is one to do with a chain? It can only throttle, choke, and enslave.

She had to struggle to free herself from the chain or she might have spent her life in the cold meshes, regarding the enigma of her father, a slave to his undefined magic. She succeeded, ultimately, in discarding him and leaving him, what was left of him, on the island, but he could not be forgotten. Unlike her mother, he had left traces and not merely traces but what could be called monuments.

He had declared his opposition to statues and memorial tablets although, it was true, he could never resist a garland and often, after a meeting that had vibrated to his speech, was as loaded as a sacrificial bull with ringed mound upon mound of rose petals, marigold, jasmine, and tinsel. The flowers were gone but she had only to smell jasmine, or marigold, for her nostrils to twitch, unbearably, with the recollection of those meetings, the roar of slogans and surge of applause.

Then there was the well in Manori — still yielding water that was sweet to the believers, brackish to the cynics. In villages near Baroda and Ahmedabad were village schools and dispensaries of which he had laid the foundation stones. His name may have been inscribed on them but she did not feel, as an adult, the inclination to go and see it, in engraved letters.

'*You* should write his biography,' one aged and mauve-faced lady in a homespun sari, the only one who had traced a line from the wan child at the edge of the dais to the married, greying Sita, had urged her. She had shrunk back as much from the suggestion as from the odour of carious teeth and the trembling of the long-boned, black-nailed fingers. 'There is no need,' she protested, for there were biographies, a row of them, written by those youthful, high-spirited, merry *chelas* of his whose talk and laughter had given the whole island house its spurious air of gaiety. The old, mauve-faced lady herself had written such a book — she presented a copy to Sita who dutifully opened it and read. Born on —, born in —, educated, ideals —, and aims —, career —, achievements —, death. Even her mother was mentioned. Married to —, it said but there was no further mention of her, or hint of her flight. His children were not left out either — a few lines were devoted to Rekha, invariably referring to her as the Nightingale of the AIR, a full paragraph to Jivan and the earliest, less inglorious, less unspeakable part of his career as a trade union leader; a single line to Sita who had not distinguished herself. The facts were dull, repetitive and, in spite of the many references to people she had known, did not interest her. Magnetic in life, after his death he seemed turned into a cold lump of metal by his biographers. None recreated his personality for her, its magic, both white and black.

What was its composition? she wondered. What were its elements? Partly, she felt, it had been his appearance — so trivial, so insignificant a part of a man, as one likes to believe, yet it had played its part. He had been ugly, grotesquely ugly, so as to arouse first notice, then pity, finally regard — a hypnotized kind of notice and regard. His heavy-lidded eyes had only briefly, flashingly shown themselves and then were so myopic as to seem piercing, fearless to the susceptible. His body was pinguid, ponderous and might have been fleshy and obese had he not known how to move his muscles and move slowly, regally, like some lion in his lair. His shoulders were so rounded as to make him seem almost hunch-backed — and that very rounded, bent attitude made him look so humble, so modest as he stood listening to the woes of the afflicted villagers or paced thoughtfully on the silver beach.

Some of the biographies contained old speeches of his and they all looked so bombastic and monotonous on the printed page that nowhere could one see why his words had drawn that band of *chelas* out onto the beach, following him, made them shout with enthusiasm and tear open their mouths and sing in fulsome praise and joy. It was true that he was not an educated man, had left school for politics when a boy, and had not taken the opportunity, as other politicians had, of long periods in jail, to acquire what is known as a self-education. He had done some reading there — those books still lay in the attic, damaged now by years of dampness and mould — the usual books of a speechmaking, non-reading politician: Emerson, John Stuart Mill, Locke, Rousseau, Hume, Thoreau and Bertrand Russell. A few oddities to redeem them from total commonplaceness — the Tibetan Book of the Dead, Kahlil Gibran, a handbook of homoeopathy. From these he had distilled that code — no one had ever analyzed the exact quantities of religious, social, and political elements that it contained — that ruled his life. He did not quote from them. His speeches were those of an uneducated man. This may, of course, have been a matter of design for he had worked mainly among the uneducated. Sita, screwing up her forehead in an effort to recall some of his words, spoken on that open, dramatic beach, could remember only a few banalities:

'See the fisherman painting his boat. Mending it. Testing it. So we should go over our hearts and heads, mending and repairing, regularly, to remain seaworthy.'

'Life is a challenge to one's instinct for self-improvement. As soon as you have grasped one rung, reach for the next...' followed, often, by a murmur of approval if not a roar of assent.

Not that every man had succumbed to his wizardry and become a *chela.* Sita had been old enough to realize, even then, that there were many who drew back and pulled strange faces as they left. When Independence was declared and he broke his longest fast to declare his intention of retiring to a village, many of his associates and colleagues who had worked with him till then, left. Sita had noticed that it was the more intelligent, the more highly educated, the sober and austere who had gone, leaving him to the young mad-cap *chelas,* most of them runaways or castaways. Some of them had quietly resumed their mundane lives as businessmen, journalists, editors, and householders: old Deedar was one of them. The island and father's experiment had made them faintly smile, shake their heads, and refuse to come.

Others, the professional politicians, had found a far more horrendous task to tackle in the partition of India and the stupefying bloodshed and violence that had erupted from the dream of independence. Shocked by the knowledge that, having taken one step forward into civilization, the country now reeled a dozen steps backward into barbarity, they had rushed to the refugee camps along the borders. Father had not chosen to follow them. Sita did not meet them in her adult life on the mainland, although she remembered some of them and also the incidents some had related about her father, sufficiently subtle to invite interpretation and yet avoided by father's biographers.

She remembered the story Deedar told of the strike and the uprising in the school where he and father had studied, on the premises of the textile mill where their parents worked. The principal had finally had one boy arrested, a firecracker, a hysterical speechmaker and ringleader of great ferocity. After much questioning and, possibly, some torture, the fact emerged that this noisy lad had nothing to do with the strike — the ringleader had been father, a boy so quiet, so withdrawn, so ugly and strange that neither the teachers nor the principal had thought him capable of organizing an incident of revolt. None of the biographers had cared to analyze that.

Then there were the incidents that Jivan had hinted at — the existence of a mistress, perhaps a second wife, and the desertion by their own mother — for Jivan was more aware of all that went on than Sita was, and had a larger imagination. Yet none of the biographers hinted at such material — they presented only the one photograph of the man whereas there had been so many. Sita knew that even though she had been too young to actually listen to him or think of his politics or his medicines. She had always been subjective in her preoccupations. Following the faithful band along the sea's edge, she had watched the sea birds settle and rock on the maternal waves, and the phosphorous that rose glinting out of the ocean as darkness descended, and had heard his voice distantly booming but paid no more attention than that.

❧

It had taken her time, therefore, to realize, that even the close band of disciples was shrinking. As she struggled through adolescence — and, deprived of a mother, a true elder sister or girl companions, she was struggled along with this infirmity as a cripple without crutches — she was plunged so deep in her own chamber, the prickling of her increasingly sensitive skin, the careless play of unaccustomed sensations, thoughts like small bats flicking through her with sharp cuts, that it took her some time to notice how small the band had grown. Where had they all gone, those many youths who had gambolled on the sand while formulating new and stupendous social revolutions; who had sat cross-legged to prayers but risen, ecstatically dancing, to devotional music? They left one after the other — promising to return, apologizing for the pressing duties that called them away, explaining the inspiration that aroused them to begin something else, somewhere else, but promising...Either they were entirely truthful or else they felt that father had cut himself off from them and gone on into a region where they, solid and down-to-earth as they basically were, could not freely breathe.

So they straggled away, not quite saying goodbye, promising vaguely to the last, till one night Sita woke and felt the impulse to once more climb the stairs to the attic where she had once spied on her father at his secret labour, she found him, not seated in the centre of a circle of *chelas,* of young men, but mostly — she blinked, pushed the hair out of her eyes disbelieving — mostly old women. Old fisherwomen they were, with boils, cataracts, tumours, and trials. A few young ones with still more intimate physical or marital disorders. So she realized as she eavesdropped, clinging to the stairhead, feeling her cotton shift blown by the salt wind, and heard him recommend strange remedies.

He leant forward, the bulky rounded shoulders threatening to topple him over, murmuring to a young woman who held her head low, hidden by a fold of her *sari,* but had one hand stretched out to receive the remedy. It was a chain, Sita saw, a common string of wooden beads. 'Take this, and with it a *mantra* — a magic *mantra* you must repeat to yourself. Here, take it,' he pressed the beads into her hand, pressed her fingers down over it and kept her rolled fist in his great hand. 'Say this, over and over again, till you are cured,' and then he leant forward still more and spoke a word which did not appear to Sita to come from any known language. Sanskrit? Possibly. Abracadabra? Also possible. She crept backwards down the stairs, clutching her hair, wondering. She had grown out of the pony stage of life, was by now a young woman, a tremendously uncertain one.

More and more, it was the women who became his newest, his latest disciples. The men kept away. Sometimes she saw curious looks on their faces as they walked past the house, glancing up at the attic with a troubled roll of their eyes, stumbling with a lack of understanding, not openly hostile but certainly anxious. The women came steadily forward for the remedies, the magic chants, the crushed jewels, the powerful pressure of his short thick fingers upon theirs. He rarely came out of the house now, or even down from the attic. He was rarely seen on the beach or, as in the beginning, out in the fields or on the village road. Increasingly invisible, he grew increasingly mysterious, already a legend that dwelt in the grey, no longer white, room above the trees.

❧

Till one night when she repeated what had become almost an act of sleepwalking, so unwilled and unplanned was it, and stood like the shadow of a tree on the top step and peered fugitively in, she saw him seated, as usual, in the dim lamplight but seated quite, quite alone. Oh, Rekha was there, as usual — but a sleepy Rekha, lying on a pallet in a dark corner, if not asleep then immobile, leaving father alone in the ring of light that encircled the mat in the centre of the unswept floor. Although he had no one at all before him, he sat in the precariously forwardleaning position that he assumed when distributing his remedies, but holding himself up by pressing his hands down on his knees. It seemed to be a strain on him to hold himself upright for his face was gashed with harsh lines, he was glistening with perspiration and his eyeballs protruded and were tinted red. He breathed stentoriously and seemed to be listening to the heavy, uneven sound. It was the attitude of a ruined lion, crouching on its haunches, appearing to be unconscious but still enigmatic enough, to create doubt and wonder.

She watched till she thought she would fall from numbness or cry out in panic. Then she forced herself to slide down the stairs to the terrace and pace there all night, holding her arms tightly around her, bare feet on the cold tiles, sobbing a little, the sound safely drowned out by the rattling of the palm leaves and the booming of the tide on the beach.

Very early, when the sky was lit with those tints of infancy — the fragile pinks and blues of the nursery — a cart came rattling up the knoll and Moses went out to meet it, still, dripping over his peacock-blue *lungi* from his morning bath by the well. Sita watched from the terrace — the tension that had gardually faded and softened with the blooming of the morning light now returning and making her rigid as she stood by the wall, frowning, puzzled by the neatly shod, neatly pressed city appearance of the youth who sprang from the cart and spoke to Moses. Moses was garrulous, kept pointing to the attic but, for some reason, kept the young man below and would not show him up. So she went slowly down the knoll to the cart, quite forgetting the lightness of the nightclothes, still clasping her arms about her and brushing through the dew-drenched weeds till she came to the bullock that happily cropped the coarse grass, and stared, waiting for him to speak.

Immediately he disentangled himself from Moses and came to her. He had come to see her father. Of course, she knew that — so she implied by a twist of her lips. His father had sent him. She raised her eyebrows, asking — who? Deedar, he said, dry-lipped — his father was Deedar. She unclasped her arms then and her lips drooped, like a child about to cry, because she thought of that kindly, portly man who used to roll up his bandanna into a mouse and make it jump about the room. She would gladly have cried then, Deedar-*dada*, Deedar-*dada*, have you brought me a mouse?

'What is it?' he asked, seeming to see how close she was to crying.

'I think he is very ill,' she said numbly. 'Come, please. He seems ill.'

That was her husband, the first she had seen of him — oddly enough, considering how well and how long she had known his father. But Deedar, a politician by logic and not by instinct, had wisely sent his children away to be brought up by some calm suburban grandmother or devoted aunt while he lived the mad life of a freedom fighter, and Sita had not known his son at all. So she maintained. He did not believe her. He said he had always known her — heard of her and, he was certain, seen her although he could not say when or where, so that she laughed, saying, 'There!' He made her laugh at a time when she had been fearfully sure that she would die along with her father on the island — how could it be otherwise?

He was dying. Myth, legend he might be but he was, physically, dying. Sita and Rekha watched him die, bit by bit. The days were wordless and grim. Sundays alone were lightened, for her, by the young man's visits. Old Deedar, himself bedridden, sent him on Sundays when he was free from business, with fruits, medicine, blankets and messages. They planned to have a doctor come, to take him away to the main land, to a hospital. He refused. He said he had his own remedies. Sita strained but saw no evidence of one. He had neither wooden beads to count, nor magic chants to mumble, nor sparkling powders to swallow. He lay on the mat on the grey floor, speechlessly staring at the tossed heads of the wind-ridden palms at the window, alone but for the two girls. The village women, having been turned away so often by Moses — at the stairs, now ceased to come. Winter drew into summer and the sea no longer dazzled but glared.

Sita realized he had died when, looking up from the mat where he lay without any apparent change in his appearance, she saw, to her astonishment, Rekha lift her heavy arms from her lap and twist her long, dishevelled hair into a tight knot at her neck with a swift, determined gesture. She stabbed one or two long pins into it, securing it, then smiled at Sita's startled, uneasy look. Her smile made Sita shrink — it was so saurian, so malevolent, cynical. Then Rekha nodded at their father, smiling, and Sita looked and saw that he had stopped breathing.

'Come,' said Rekha, in a voice that rang, 'we can go now.'

She went, immediately, as though she had waited for and planned for this moment of release from the old man's love. She seemed to know exactly what to do, whom to go to. It was a matter of months before she became the Nightingale of AIR and people, earlyrisers sipping their first cup of tea or meditatively brushing their teeth, turned the knobs of their radios to tune in to her voice singing a morning hymn with that absolutely clear, utterly certain voice of a goddess.

Jivan had disappeared some time ago. He had been the first — Sita now realized — to see that her father was ill, dying. He had left astutely, at the very moment of realization. She heard of him next when he had become a headline-maker, a turbulent trade union leader always in the knotted centre of troubles and riots. Since he had become one of those who cannot afford to hold an address, a telephone number or any traceable designation she never saw him again.

She herself would have stayed on, in the deserted house, for she had not planned anything, had not understood the need to plan or plot or prepare and was quite destitute. She contemplated, numbly, staying on alone into old age out of not knowing what else could be done with one's long life, too long life, when Deedar's son came to cremate her father, shut the house, fetch her away, send her to college, install her in a college hostel and finally — out of pity, out of lust, out of sudden will for adventure, and because it was inevitable married her.

She always remembered how he had set down, on the terrace, the basket and the rolled rug that made up all her luggage, swung the two leaves of the front door together and put a lock on the bolt, then turned to hand the key, with a worried look of misgiving, to Moses, before he took her down the steps to the waiting bullock cart. He looked exactly like a tired manager drawing the curtains together, locking up the empty theatre with its cigarette stubs and stale odours and dust, and stepping out on to the street. It was as though he had been expressly sent by providence to close the theatrical era of her life, her strange career, and lead her out of the ruined theatre into the thin sunlight of the ordinary, the everyday, the empty and the meaningless.

She had left with relief, worn out by the drama of Manori, longing for the sane, the routine-ridden mainland as for a rest in a sanatorium. It was only gradually, as the light of the ordinary world grew stiff, static and petrified around her, as the streets and walls ceased to offer security or safety but implied threats of murder instead, that she once again began to think of the island. She saw its shape again, that dark saucer on the steel pale sea, white birds suddenly rising to swoop across its breadth, and Moses' small boat setting out from the rusty coast to fetch her back into its ring of magic.

He had been a wizard, she accepted that now, her father. He had cast an illusion as a fisherman casts a net, with the faintest sussuration of warning, upon a flock of fish in the sea. His *chelas* were the first to be caught, then the villagers, most inescapably the women. His wife had torn a hole in the net and escaped into the dark depths of the ocean. The others he had held in his net and smiled upon, most inscrutably. Fed them with pearls, caressed their long hair, fondled their fingers, whispered magic chants into their ears and then, as he lay dying, released them, saint-like into their native sea.

Knowing that, accepting that, she knew it was because ordinary life, the everyday world had grown so insufferable to her that she could think of the magic island again as of release. If the sea was so dark, so cruel, then it was better to swim back into the net. If reality were not to be borne, then illusion was the only alternative. She saw that island illusion as a refuge, a protection. It would hold her baby safely unborn, by magic. Then there would be the sea — it would wash the frenzy out of her, drown it. Perhaps the tides would lull the children, too, into smoother, softer beings. The grove of trees would shade them and protect them.

'To Manori,' she so promptly said, then, in answer to her husband's habitual summer query, 'Where shall we go this summer?'

part three

monsoon '67

The monsoon flowed — now thin, now dense; now slow, now fast; now whispering, now drumming; then gushing. There was never silence — always the roar and sigh of the tide, the moan of the casuarinas in the grove below, tossed and hurled about in grey, tattered billows, the clatter of palm leaves that hung their ragged fingers down and made channels for the rain to spout down onto the roof. The children stared about them with great, afraid eyes and spoke only to point out, bitterly, another leak in the roof, or a whole window frame comes loose from its hinges. It was clear they accused her of every mishap and misfortune. Whenever she turned or looked up, she saw them staring at her, watching her as though waiting for her to break down and admit failure. To them, she realized with a painful sloughing-off of disbelief, it was life in their flat on Napean Sea Road that had been right and proper, natural and acceptable; it was this so called 'escape' to the island that was madness.

It can't go on like this, it's impossible! She cried everyday, several times a day, in a choked voice that fought speechlessness at the grotesquerie of their situation. She wanted to explain to them that it had not been madness to come, had not been a theatrical gesture, a romantic mistake. Romantic — rubbish! She protested, flushing — Manori was not a romantic island.

Besides its palms, its deserted beach, its wild silence, there was that most squalid of villages, with its open drains, its mangy *pai* dogs, drunkards. The atmosphere of that fishing village, of which Moses and Miriam, too, reeked, penetrated her own knoll, her palm grove and even the house: the continual wash of the rain could not quite cleanse it. Moses, stalking, cut with yet another lantern he had kicked over and broken, and Miriam, sitting on her haunches and smoking a cigar, saying with more insolence than despair, 'But there is nothing to cook!' made her remember those two vivid creatures, the 'original inhabitants' of *Jeevan Ashram,* dressed in throbbing shades of pink and orange. Seeing them as they were now, bloated into two heavy purple presences like two aubergines on legs, she was confused — where *was* the magic of the island that she had promised herself, promised the children? Was *this* it?

If it had ever existed — black, sparkling and glamorous as in her memory — it was now buried beneath the soft grey-green mildew of the monsoon, chilled and choked by it. It was all the children saw, they had no memory of its past glamour, and so she and they moved always in opposite directions. Round and round that ruined house they stalked, hemmed in by rain and sea, clockwise and counter-clockwise and, whenever their paths crossed, every half-hour or so, they accused her in silence and she pleaded with them, in silence too.

In the veranda, the bucket she had put out overflowed. She ran out to fetch it in and was, briefly, pleased and wet. She had forbidden Miriam to draw water from the well after discovering that Ali's cow had fallen into it and drowned.

'And *not* been taken out?' she had gasped; and taken to putting out buckets to collect the rain. Karan had begged her to let him go and see the cow floating, swollen, in the well. Even Menaka — she could tell from a cool shift of her eyes — would not have minded. 'No!' she had forbidden them. Carrying the bucket into the kitchen she wondered what they could do with it — they could not have it for lunch.

Miriam still squatted there, smoking. 'There is nothing to cook,' she repeated, sulkily. 'Fishermen don't go out in monsoon time.'

'Cook another jackfruit then,' Sita said weakly, and dared not answer her children when they asked, 'What's for lunch?' She knew perfectly well what they thought of jackfruit.

They sat together, watching and listening to the occasional softening and paling of the rain and then its growing wilder, denser again. But, as it thinned that morning, allowing the palms and casuarinas to lift a little and the view of the far wall to stand out of the wet haze, a figure detached itself from the casuarina grove, came up the path with bowed head but steady feet, up the stairs to the veranda, and Sita, standing up to watch, remembered how she had twined herself about a freshly painted white pillar to see the village folk come up that path, in winter sunshine, with flat baskets on their heads containing offerings for her father — green coconuts in bunches, pink shrimps fresh from the sea with a giant lobster or two wriggling beneath them, or paper roses, pink and yellow. Remembering them, the festivity and affection in the air around them, she opened the door now and called, 'Who are you?'

It was a fisherwoman — one could tell by the way her drenched *sari* was pulled up between her legs and tucked in at the waist, by her spread feet and enormous toes made for gripping the fishing lines and nets of her trade. An old woman, with cataract lurking in one eye like a white fish. She lifted the flat basket off her head and placed it on the floor at Sita's feet. Sita drew back, hissing with astonishment, for the basket crawled with shrimps — pink and infantile, their transparent whiskers aquiver, emanating a stench that called, that shouted *we live, we are shrimps!* Karan ran forward to examine them and poke them and, from the way his face expanded and glowed, it seemed as though this were the first sign of life he had encountered on this island of the dead.

'You are Babaji's daughter,' the old woman said in a Konkani dialect as raw and harsh as wet fishing lines. 'I brought oil for Babaji once, and coconuts, and he blessed me with a son. So I have brought something for you today.'

'What is your name?'

'Phoolmaya,' said the old woman, suddenly splitting open into a yellow smile.

Phoolmaya — Sita stared at her. She had been beautiful, lying on the floor with her arms, silver with bracelets, streched out to touch her father's feet. She did not wish to refer to that age or that scene; it would be ludicrous and cruel to try to link them to the woman who stood there, grinning. 'How did you know I am here?' she asked instead.

'Moses told. Now I will tell in the village. They will all bring you fish.'

'How is your son?' Sita asked, not knowing how to thank her, feeling shamefully weak and ravenous to think of food, proper food, being brought and cooked.

'A big man,' the woman said with almost voluptuous satisfaction. 'Will you give me tobacco? Babaji always gave me tobacco.'

Sita went to fetch some cigars from Miriam and found Karan and Menaka squatting on the kitchen threshold, laughing as they watched Miriam who sat with her thighs spread out and the basket between her legs, tearing the transparent shells off the pink, trembling bodies of the infant shrimps. 'Fish fry today,' laughed Miriam, feeling in her blouse for some cigars.

After that, almost everyday, whenever the rain slowed or there was a short break, luminous and pure, in the monsoon, people came from the fishing village, over the beach, carrying full baskets as they had done in that other, magical age. With such concrete evidence as a vessel of milk, a cluster of hibiscus, a moss-covered crab or a lobster to point at, Sita found herself clasping Karan's shoulder, almost shaking him, as she said, 'See, didn't I tell you?' It was clear even to the child that it was herself she was shaking, clasping, persuading. She had herself almost ceased to believe in magic, in life, in animation.

The monsoon continued like an unceasing burial. There was nothing to do with it but watch it, listen to it, sighing at the window. Very soon her cigarettes ran out. The last ones had been too damp to light and she had thrown them out, quite ashamed of the agony this waste caused her. Seeing her sit so desolate after this act of violence, Miriam — in the first burst of sensitivity ever revealed — suddenly bared her bright pink gums in a laugh and crowed, 'Amma, you have no cigarettes left. I shall make you some!' Sufficiently abject to succumb, Sita sat watching as Miriam pulled up her skirt over her great thighs and rolled the soft leaves of tobacco from her pouch on them, leering up at Sita as she did so, then handing her suprisingly neat and slim brown cigarillos with an odour Sita could not resist. They were too thick to fit into her old yellowed ivory cigarette holder so she threw that away and tasted the tobacco direct on her lips, as she sat down to pull at the first with an indrawn breath of gratitude.

'Oh my dears,' she said, emotionally, to the children who sat dully watching as she dragged on that cigarillo with a white passion of satisfaction, 'when I am on my death bed, hold one of Miriam's cigars under my nose. If I don't leap up to snatch it from you, you can coolly go ahead and burn me.'

Then she stopped short, horrified at her mistake — this succumbing to a moment of adult pleasure, adult talk, in the company of children — for Menaka turned away, her face clenched with displeasure.

It was not that Menaka feared her death — not at all; but there had been a time when the idea of death had been unbearable, unacceptable to her. Looking at her,. contrite, Sita remembered what she had been like as a small child, of

Karan's age or smaller — a girl in a white cotton nightgown, after her bath, powdered, sweet, curled up in bed and crying in the dark. So loved, so carefully laid in bed but crying, 'Will they put you in the ground? When you are dead, will they put you in the ground?' Comforting her hopelessly — for what comfort was there? When she was dead she would not be put in the ground, no, but burnt to ashes and how could she tell the little girl that? Sita had searched for the cause of this sudden agony and remembered walking hand-in-hand with her through an old English cemetery on a weekend visit to Lonavla in the hills, and seeing Menaka's eyes rest on those white headstones scattered about the coarse grass and tumbled rocks of the hillside below their cottage, as her mind stored away its memory and some fluttering, bat-like thoughts that she did not then express and had so led her mother to think she had forgotton them. She had not. For some years then death occupied her and terrified her as it should not any but the doomed, and Sita had been too incompetent a mother to know how to deal with her trauma, how to give her comfort — there was none, and it was not in her to concoct any.

She need not have suffered so much anxiety though for Menaka had grown into the most cool and self-possessed of her children, most closely resembling her father in her ability to cope with life and accept it with no more than a careless shrug of the shoulders. By the time she was ten — a supercilious, self-contained, and beautiful young girl — she had made up her mind to be a doctor and watched a student cousin dissect a mouse with an intense and dispassionate curiosity that sickened and inflamed her mother. Watching that unappetising scene, Sita had been shocked at the transition from the small, weeping infant to this calm scientist.

So she knew it was not fear that made her grimace and turn away from her mother: it was disapproval. Menaka — the calm, reasonable scientist to be — this Menaka loathed her mother's proclivity for drama, for theatre, for emotion, with more bitterness than any other suffering relation of hers. Being her daughter, she felt most disgusted and hurt by it.

Ashamed, hurt, Sita leant forward and touched her arm, pleadingly, lightly. 'Menaka,' she coaxed, knowing she was only making matters worse, and Menaka winced and shook off her hand.

'What is it?' she said impatiently.

Sita leant back, the cigarillo tasting of black ashes now, nothing more. She had grown very large and heavy and tired easily, now. 'Look,' she said, 'at that crow sheltering in the veranda. Poor thing, how wet and sorry it looks.'

Only Karan went to the window to look at it, Menaka would not. Quite possibly, Sita reflected, that scene she had made with the pop-gun over the wounded eagle would put Menaka off any pity, any feeling for birds forever. Children were like that, Sita sighed. Leaving Menaka alone, she turned to Karan. 'Why don't you play?' she asked when she felt he had stood an unnaturally long time at the window, staring at the bedraggled crow.

'What shall I play?' he asked, without his sister's sulkiness but with as much despair at this exile she had led him into.

Blowing out white smoke, spitting out stray bits of tobacco, Sita tried seriously to think of an answer, 'We used to play,' she said, distantly, 'Jivan and I — such games on the beach, together.'

'But he can't go out in the rain,' said Menaka sharply.

'What did you play?' Karan came to stand near her. She made room for him to sit down beside her and put her arms around him in gratitude. She tried to make the telling of the games she had played as a child amusing for him, colourful, and knew all along that she had no gift for narrative at all.

To be truthful, she had no more gifts for play than he seemed to have. It was Jivan who invented the games and organized them with a ferocity touched with genius. He insisted always that they play in secret — in some weed-screened corner of the casuarina grove where no one could spy them, or among the rocks on the beach when no one was about. The games had been elaborate.

'One game was called Funerals —' she began, then stopped, for she remembered, too late, that she had once again used the tabooed word.

'What is that?' he inevitably asked.

She avoided a straight answer, even though she knew Menaka was watching her with hate and enmity. She told him how they would collect bits of wood on the beach and light a bonfire and burn a large bivalve shell in it, or a crab's claw found in a pool, and then cast the blackened remains into the sea.

'Processions — that was another,' she smartly, quickly continued, and told him how they had made garlands with the flowering bindweed from the sand dunes and climbed onto rocks and made speeches. Then sung the national anthem and screamed the freedom movement slogans with which they were so familiar. She demonstrated all this to Karan who hopped up, then flopped down with his knees tucked under his chin and devoured with hungry eyes this passage of animation, of unaccustomed fun. It inspired him to go and find a rag and wave it as a flag above his head, stamp his feet and shout out loud for the first time since he had come to Manori. She watched his pale performance, thinking of the way Jivan used to play the same game — not with the excitement and passion she had poured into them and of which her son now performed a weak, pathetic copy — but with a total commitment that completely altered him and saved her. Put the wood here — strike a match — bring the garland — now sing — no, I'll sing — he would command and work it all out with precision and power. No unexpected element ever dismayed him. If someone stumbled upon their game, he would carry on calmly, only imperceptibly altering his words and actions to make it seem he was giving a lecture or demonstration to his sister rather than being involved in it himself.

Karan had already tired of the game, was back at the window, looking out at the rain that stood as sound and solid as an asbestos sheet about them. Even the woebegone crow was gone drowning or drowned in the rain. Even the sea could not be heard for the rush of the rain, the frenzied lashing and beating of the palm leaves about them. Something slammed and crashed into splinters — in one of the outhouses or in the derelict attic upstairs.

Sita felt a spasm of fear at her bravado, her wild words, her impulsive actions that had flung them alone onto this island surrounded by wild seas. It was no place in which to give birth. There was no magic here — the magic was gone. She laid her hand protectively on her swelling stomach. What if, as her husband had warned, something happened? For all her inspired words, she knew she could not shelter it inside her forever. And who was there to help when the time of parting came — Miriam? At the thought of Miriam's burly arms plunging into her, handling the fragile skull of the infant with her fat, smacking hands, Sita felt ill and rolled her head about the cushion, trying to drive away the blood-tinted picture. Her escapade was becoming too like one of those horror stories that appear in newspapers, of women giving birth in tree-tops during floods, in the middle of an earthquake, or inside an aeroplane. The more physical details of the matter crowded her mind. Usually she repressed them with an agonized determination but the rain drumming, thrumming, pouring all about her locked her in, locked her up, forced her to turn on herself.

'Menaka!' she shouted, sitting up, her hair all tormented. 'Menaka! Karan!'

They appeared, for once, immediately like spectres she had summoned out of the rain — so pale, so peaked, both of them, their hair grown long and thin, hanging in wisps about their white cheeks and dull eyes. 'Stay with me,' she begged, her pity for herself flooding out into a vast pity for them, making her open her arms wide to draw them to her. Obediently they sat beside her. Karan placed his hand on her lap, then let her pick him up and hold him. She held him close, kissed the nape of his neck, then turned to smile at Menaka and reach out for her hand. 'Let's play together,' she begged. 'Karan, if you fetch some mud in your bucket, we could do some modelling, Menaka, help him.'

Later in the afternoon Miriam came to make them tea and found Sita on the floor with Karan, the pail of mud overturned between them, chuckling and laughing as she helped him roll and pat and mould and stack it in childish shapes. Some of it stuck to her hair and stained her clothes but she was oblivious of that as she happily patted and shaped it and laughed over it.

For some reason Miriam restrained her yell of astonishment, then her fat hand rose automatically and she crossed herself and silently backed out.

Sita felt the same oblivious joy when she came upon Menaka, one day, doing a pastel sketch in her room sitting by the window, her bare foot propped up on the ledge, the drawing board slanting across her slim thighs, her hair tied up in a knot on her neck with a blue cotton handkerchief that cast across her cheek a soft, mauve shadow. The joy of seeing Menaka thus occupied, thus beautifully occupied, made her too oblivious, too incautious, too impulsive again.

The third time she opened the door to peep in proved too much. For all her contained poise, her smooth inward stance, Menaka was upset. She threw the board down on its face with a bang and sat there, clenching the window ledge with her toes.

'What's the matter?' Sita asked, shocked by the sight of the pastel sketch face-downward on the floor.

Menaka got up and stood with her back to the window. Her lips were so thin, her eyes so narrowed, Sita felt she was about to explode into a passion just as she herself did. She did not. She kicked the board into a corner and said, carelessly, 'Nothing.'

'You've spoilt your picture!'

'It was spoilt already.'

'Oh let me see,' Sita hurried to turn over the board and rescue the sketch but Menaka got there first, tore off the paper and shredded it violently. Sita felt her heart beating and leaping sideways at all this violence that she herself had ignited. 'Why did you tear it?'

'I'm *bored* with it,' Menaka snapped.

'Don't you enjoy sketching, Menaka? I thought you did.'

'I only do it when there's nothing else to do. When I'm bored. There's nothing else to do here.' Accusations shot out from her like so many pellets from a burst cartridge.

'What would you like to do?' Sita spoke to her softly, as to an agitated bird she was trying to hold in hand and soothe, calm, not knowing it was the very touch of her hand that drove the bird wild.

'I wish I were back in school. I wish it were time to join college. It *is* nearly time.'

Sita sighed and turned to the bed and began smoothing the sheets and tucking the corners in. 'Yes, we must think about college now, I suppose. What will you study, Menaka? Have you thought—'

'Science,' Menaka shot at her, still with her back to the window, her lips thin, her eyes fierce, narrow. 'I've told you that before,' she added.

'You've told me before,' Sita agreed, nodding, and put a finger into a hole in the sheet. 'But that was when you were smaller. I wondered if you had changed your mind or if you felt quite certain—'

'I am certain.'

'But, Menaka, what about your painting? You paint so *well,* Menaka.'

'It's only a hobby,' the girl said impatiently, shaking her head, abruptly, rejecting art with that one rough shake.

'Only a hobby,' Sita repeated, wondering. Then she sat down on Menaka's bed — it was a matter of marvel how she unfailingly made the wrong moves, knowing them to be wrong yet making them as if there were nothing else she could do — and lit one of Miriam's dark and powerful cigarillos. She had not noticed yet how the sight and smell of them revolted the fastidious girl. 'I always thought — if you only took it more seriously — not as a hobby — but studied it — you could make it your career. I mean, of course, if you *wanted* to.'

'I don't want to. I shall be a scientist.'

'Oh, *science,* Menaka!' Sita's knee jerked nervously. 'Science can't be as satisfactory. It's all — all figures, statistics, logic. Science is believing that two and two make four — pooh,' she exhaled a mouthful of acrid smoke in blatant disgust.

'What else can it be?' Menaka exclaimed, spontaneously for once.

'Why, anything. Three — or five. You're not taking into account that one part of the two may be a shrunk, shrivelled thing, the other a fat and swollen thing that overshadows it.'

'But,' cried Menaka in amazement, 'the very fact that the numbers are alike means that their quantities are alike.'

'Pooh —' out shot another mouthful of rocking smoke. 'That is this absurd method of labelling. A label doesn't reveal the quality.'

'What *does* it reveal then?'

'Nothing, nothing. It's a mask, a shroud, nothing else. It leads you to a dead-end. There are no dead ends, now, in art. That is something spontaneous, Menaka, and alive, and creative...'

Menaka lost interest — she had heard that argument too often. Arguments with her mother always ended in this kind of haze, of obscurity and nonsense that her trim and practical self loathed instinctively. 'That's all nonsense,' she muttered, turning around to the window, looking out at the rain. 'I can't stand nonsense. It's boring.'

'And art is nonsense?'

'Mostly.'

'Oh Menaka,' Sita sighed, spilling ash on the floor sadly. 'I wish I had your talent. I would nurse it so carefully — like a plant — make it grow, grow. I used to think — after I left this island and had to think what I would do next — that if only I could paint, or sing, or play the *sitar* well, really well, I should have grown into a sensible woman. Instead of being what I am,' she said with stinging bitterness, rubbing the ash this way and that with her slipper. 'I should have known how to channel my thoughts and feelings, how to put them to use. I should have given my life some shape then, some meaning. At least, it would have had some for me — even if no one else had cared.'

Menaka ostentatiously displayed her lack of interest, keeping her back turned to her mother, her face to the streaming rain. Sita added, 'I used to think that — I still believe that,' but what she thought and said did not interest Menaka, stubbornly did not interest Menaka. Menaka would don white overalls and stand in a laboratory, pouring a known quantity of chemical from one tube to another, noting down its quantity and quality in a neat register. She would label the tubes, calculate the results, and all about her, in that white, metallic hall, there would be logic, order, sense. She had had enough of her mother's disorder and nonsense — she would escape it wholly.

She moved from there only to exclaim, with a sudden change of tone, 'Miriam's after Karan again!' and left the room hurriedly to rescue her brother, Sita being now too slow and too tired to move quickly enough.

A major part of Karan's life on the island was taken up in hiding or escaping from the attentions of Miriam. He looked quite piqued, Sita noticed, from the effort of running away from the bulbous Miriam who had once, when he had slithered down the knoll to gaze at her goats in the drizzle, caught him in her arms, more fit to grapple with a python than caress a child and, smacking her lips over him as over a tasty snack, raucously bawled—

Don't cry, baby, don't cry,
    Mama making chilli fry,
Papa catching butterfly,
    Don't cry, baby, don't cry.

then flung him in the air, caught him and was about to smack his mouth with her loose lips when Menaka, stopping swiftly and quietly, came down from the kitchen and put Miriam in her place with an icy look of disapproval and brought Karan back to the house that seemed so like a jail to both of them, surrounded by the barbed wire of ceaseless raindrops.

Sita was left on the bed, smoking, rubbing her toes in the ash, feeling them draw away from her, into other regions, regions safer and duller, shutting themselves in with the barbed wire of prudence, caution, routine and order, leaving her in her own disorderly region that smelt of raw tobacco, was lashed by the monsoon storm that swept so freely over the desolate island, leaving her there out of disapproval, horror even, and an instinctive rejection of her wild values and wild searches, leaving her. She lay back on the bed and shut her eyes.

Then there was a break in the monsoon — one of those breaks that come when one has resigned oneslf to it, resigned oneself to the thought that it will rain forever and one will wallow always in water. Then the solidity of the cloud ceiling showed cracks — rifts of soft white, rifts of weakness — that widened into pale channels so that the clouds separated at last, drifted free, became light enough for the wind to send them floating this way and that.

Sita and the children went out on the terrace to watch the massed clouds, kohl-black, floating and shifting, now engulfing, now releasing the sky, casting a shadow over the slaty sea, turning it to a trough of green-black chill, then moving on to let a shaft of white sunlight stream down and scatter its dull silver coins upon the waves. The clouds did not mass together again — they remained loose, buoyant and, early one morning when the sky was flushed and the palms black smudges on its pink pastel tints, the fishing fleet set gallantly out. From the terrace they watched the triangles of white sails move in and out of the islands of light, now traversing a grim cloud-shadow, now chasing and skipping after a spangle of light. It was not the full fleet — only a few boats sailed by men who could not bear another idle day in the cramped, sodden huts of the village. They had an air of being out for adventure rather than business.

Overjoyed by their wit, their gallantry, their briskness, Sita ignored the fine, passing drizzle, ignored Menaka's warning, 'Karan will catch cold,' and led them down the stone steps from the terrace to the grove. 'We'll go out on the beach today,' she vowed. Karan ran ahead of her. Even Menaka began to look about her a little, notice things, trivial things. Sita smiled at her in gratitude, laughed when Karan sprang backwards, having nearly stepped on a frog, and pointed out the wildflowers to them.

Crowding about them in well-watered lushness were squat and leafy *cheekoo* trees, dense and burly and knotted with small fruit — 'We'll pluck them and ripen them in a bag of rice,' Sita promised Karan who was eyeing them — drumstick trees with their long beans and twisted garlands of small orchid-like flowers, tattered palms and palmyras, bushes of hibiscus and lantana in bloom. The earth seethed with weeds and the weeds with minute wildflowers in brilliant tints — waxy white stars, curled yellow ones, small blue eyes and clusters of vermilion and coral ixora that Sita plucked and scattered for the pleasure of smelling their sweet, tarry sap on her hands. Butter-yellow and kingfisher-blue butterflies flew up like so many petals taking flight.

In the pond down by the outhouses, buffaloes bathed luxuriously, with a dull-gleaming Roman opulence in the roll of their eyes and their heavy expressions, while green frogs leapt from one slick hide to the other. Karan would have liked to stay and watch them, throwing pebbles, but Sita drove him down through the grove.

'We'll go to the sea today,' she insisted, but stopped short herself when she came upon a battered, bowed, crippled old fig tree by the gate from which an old rope hung in a loop. Moses had tied it — not this Moses but another, a handsome, youthful, good-humoured Moses who had smelt only incidentally of liquor — to make her a swing. Entranced, she stood in the weeds, gazing at it, and saw herself as that young girl with long, streaming hair who had hitched herself up on that loop and swung forwards to the sea, swung backwards to the white house on the knoll, swung out to the dazzling sea, swung back, swung forwards, swung, swung — swung herself dizzy, swung herself sick, swung herself down in a tumbled heap in the weeds.

'What are you staring at?' Karan demanded impatiently, shrilly. 'You said we'd play in the sea.'

'Come then,' she said, placing her hand on his shoulder, and they went out through the broken gate, down a flight of stone steps that the rain had washed clean of sand and, stepping out of the fringed shadows of the casuarinas and across the tangle of bindweed on the dunes, were out on the beach.

The wind there blowed along cold and free. It slapped them sharply, with chilly smacks that made the women hold their hair down about their ears and Karan leap high with laughter. It whipped up small waves on the darkly gleaming sea and some invisible sunshine, emerging from round the corners of round and friendly clouds, edged each wave with shining steel. The sand glittered too, in this concealed light, and was smoother than the sea. Barefoot, they ran along the edge of the sea and the waves rushed up to meet them, then turned and retreated, leaving a dazzle of phosphorescent bubbles on the shining sand.

Karan ran and tumbled at a drunken pace. The sudden expansion of the world, its unexpected spaciousness, seemed to go to his head in one swift draught. Then he discovered the infinite detail into which it split, this massed treasure, and stopped at every pool and puddle between the jagged rocks from which locks of tumbled seaweed hung. He climbed the rocks, sharp with limpets, to look into the pools where crabs scuttled past, only their claws visible outside their shells, at the shiny black mussels and glassy shrimps timidly putting out their whiskers and then hastily burrowing out of sight again. He pulled out handfuls of bladder-wrack and squashed the soft, gassy bladders. He screamed as something heaved beneath his foot and jumped aside to let an angry crab, camouflaged by its green carapace, scuttle away. Sita showed him some small anemones in a shallow rock pool and he watched their tentacles close about the stick she poked at them with a disbelief that made her laugh. They knelt on the wet sand, watching the exquisite tentacles furl and unfurl and till the sandhoppers made their legs itch and burn and they went further down the beach at a run.

'Let's go out on that,' Menaka said, pointing at a long, thin arm of land that went a furlong into the sea. They found it crisply encrusted with shells, broken and whole, white and twinkling with them, and Menaka bent down and collected tellins and periwinkles and wondered if there were a conch. A group of gulls that were resting on the tip of the sandbar flew up, crying with alarm, then settled at a little distance, on the rocking waves, quite as calmly and comfortably as though on their own nests.

They walked along, their feet crunching the brittle powder of crushed shells, now and then stabbed or cut by the sharp edge of a whole shell or a concealed rock. 'Look,' said Sita, bending to show them how shells seemed always to search for security, attaching themselves to a stone, there forming layer on crusted layer, or to a strand of seaweed, clinging to it like so many pearls to a string. 'My bracelet,' she said, winding a strand about her wrist and pretended not to see, although she glowed, Menaka doing the same.

Karan found something too — 'Look!' he yelled, with all the pride of a discoverer: it was something small, round, porous in texture, creamy in colour, punctured at the two sides. 'Ugh, it's a bone — throw it away,' Sita said and made him fling it into the sea. His jerky movement made the gulls on the water bridle and scold like agitated matrons, then settle down to their rocking again.

The wind rose out of the sea and dashed spray against them. 'It's beginning to rain,' Menaka shouted but Sita said,

'It's only spray' and went further out into the sea till she was brought up short by the sight of something strange and glaucous stranded on the tip of the sandbar. They approached it with caution, stood a little away from it, and it was some time before Sita could inform them, 'It's a jellyfish.' The children went closer, Karan squatted, his knees sticking up about his ears bonily, and brought himself to poke it with a stick.

Sita remained at a distance and regarded the creature, spilling across the shell-scattered sandbar, reflectively and with some surprise at finding it, in the end, not horrifying so much as sad. It resembled so little anything that had ever breathed or moved. It appeared to her to be the brain or the opaque 'mind' of some gigantic undersea creature that had lived all its life far beneath the level where light penetrated and that had, in the creature's tormented death pangs, burst forth from the fine white skull — washed and washed again to that unearthly whiteness — and risen to the surface of the sea, but quickly surrendered its few moments of momentum to the wash and draw of the waves. Tossed up and thrown onto the sandbar by the discarding waves, it now lay quite still again as it had inside the skull of that mostly passive and unadventurous sea creature, for Sita's eyes to regard till a sudden pulsing movement inside her reminded her of the foetus stranded between her hips and she was startled by the similarity of what floated inside her, mindless and helpless, to this poor washed thing thrown onto the beach, opaque and wet and sad.

'Come, let's turn back,' she said fearfully and dragged Karan to his feet and drew him away, reluctantly, then followed him and Menaka very slowly with her arms folded about her and her head bowed low.

❧

The days swung by to a slower pace now — the lazy, idle, leisurely pace of a relief, a lull. The soft opalescence of the seaside mornings with their infant tints of blue and pink and milk-grey would harden gradually into the heavy, glittering metal of the stiff afternoons when they lay resting, dozing in the shade of palm leaves that seemed cut out of sheet metal. Evening would rustle up through the casuarinas, clatter the palm leaves together and start up a murmur of pleasure, of animation, in the house, on the knoll and out on the beach. Sita would walk barefoot on the wet sand and the children would bathe in the sea which, although churned and tormented by the monsoon storms till it was muddy and full of long, floating seaweed ripped from the seabed, was calm now, as if exhausted by the storms. They bathed till the sun turned mellow, turned liquid, flowed into the sea, leaving the sky pink and blue and tender again. The wind whipped up cold and Sita hurried to wrap towels about the wet and streaming children, then led them up through the grove, stopping to point out to them the lighted flares with which the villagers were out hunting crabs on the rocks, up onto the knoll where Moses was lighting the lamps — soft, golden kerosene lamps for their house and hot, harsh Petromaxes for his.

How long would it continue like this, she wondered, pacing on the terrace at night when the children were asleep. If it stayed like this long enough, without a disturbance, without an interruption, perhaps the slowness, the monotony of the regular tides would enter one's very veins, one's blood would begin to flow to their measure and one would adjust to a life in which there was never any change but the expected one of the tide receding and the tide advancing. A lulled life, half-conscious, dream-like. Even the unborn child might adjust to a life that would live itself out in the warm, even tides of her womb and never create a storm, scream and severe itself. Was it possible? She wondered, pacing the terrace at night. It seemed not impossible on those nights on the terrace that she spent alone.

Nor was she lonely. Even when the children were away, playing or asleep — and they intruded strangely little on her consciousness considering how much and how close together they were in that isolated house — she never felt alone. She felt surrounded by presences — the presence of the island itself, of the sea around it, and of the palm trees that spoke to each other and, sometimes, even to her. They were so alive. In the beginning they had seemed harsh, rattling their oversized, brittle leaves together as if in warning, or disapproval; standing on one charred leg each, offering a minimum of shade or greenery. Yet, for all their stiffness and dryness, she came to see how extraordinarily responsive they were to every nuance of light and air, how alive. The breeze could make the leaves patter to sound like the approach of sweet raindrops, or shake them to sound like a downpour, or rattle them — one by one, suddenly, explosively, like a nightjar uttering its sudden, loud squawks.

The noonday light on them turned them to sheet metal — metallic, dazzling in the unequivocal light. Moonlight silvered them romantically, with a pale, silken sheen. Every moment of the day or night they stood there, responding to the elements differently, curiously, so that really they were not stiff at all but so responsive, so alive as to seem birds rather than vegetables — stiff-legged, tough-feathered cranes that sleep with one eye open, always prepared to spread their wings, squawk and hiss.

So Sita never felt alone or unsafe; the house in its grove of palms, seemed surrounded by a host of watchful cranes, always half-awake, ready to spring to life at the slightest touch or alteration in light and wind, raise their wings and give voice to warning. The grove was like a radar system planted around her house. At times she almost feared it and then unquiet heaved inside her again.

Beginning to pace up and down, up and down, she would strain to catch the precise language of this invisible unquiet. 'Where shall we go this summer?' The words, appearing out of nowhere; worried her and plagued her. 'Nowhere, nowhere,' she made an effort to control herself and quietly reply. 'I'll keep you safe inside. We'll go nowhere.' Soothing herself, reassuring herself, she silenced the doubts and walked more slowly till there entered into her mind again those wavering, disconnected lines she still could not place or capture:

. . .even the slumbrous egg as it labours
    under the shell
Patiently to divide and sub-divide. . . .

Of course it rained again. The monsoon was not over — it had merely been resting. It came back, fold on fold of cloud, roll on roll of thunder. But now it did not oppress her and batter her: she knew it would ebb away and sink into the sea to wait till next summer, next year.

Then Moses came through the storm, shouting with excitement, holding down a triangle of sacking over his head, his fat thighs wobbling as he pushed his way up through the rain. He stood streaming with wet and with self-importance on the veranda and shouted to be heard above the din of the rain on the roof, '*Sahib* is coming! *Sahib* is coming!'

She felt one violent pulsation of grief inside her, like a white bird flying up with one strident scream, then plummeting down, thinking, 'It's all over —' and then a warm expansion of relief, of pleasure, of surprise — oh happy surprise! She began to laugh for the children were already shouting, 'When? When? Has he come?' Everything stirred, tumbled, rose around her. Strange, she thought — the man so passive, so grey, how could the very mention of him arouse such a tumult of life and welcome. She felt it herself — unwillingly, unexpectedly — but she felt it.

'The driver came to Marve,' Moses said. 'He left a message at the tea-shop: *Sahib* will come tomorrow, after office.'

As the time approached for him to come — Moses had set out in the boat early for it was raining and the short distance from the island to the mainland could be covered only slowly and with some skill — Sita's agitation grew. The thought of his adult, quiet, critical company gave her a sense of sharp pleasure. But the sight of the childrens' almost unbearable excitement dashed cold water on her delight. She thought, bitterly, that they were being disloyal to her, disloyal to the island and its wild nature. She went into her room and shut the door on their giddy, whirling excitement and then — strangest of all — felt rising in her a positive cyclone of feminine instinct, a mental reckoning of the clothes she had with her, preferring this, rejecting that, seeing herself thus. Then, with a swift onslaught of shame, she rejected such thoughts and did not change, on purpose, but kept on her oldest and drabbest sari and left her hair as it was. Before she could change her mind again, she heard Karan shout frantically 'Papa! Papa!' and from the window saw him rush down the knoll in the drizzle, with a kind of despair in his outflung arms and bent knees as if he feared he would not catch his father but be left in the dark house on this empty island.

Oddly enough when Raman came up the veranda steps and saw her standing in the doorway, he too thought first of all of her dress. He had always been dismayed by the extravagance of her dress. It was something that disconcerted all her acquaintances — for it was not that she was extravagant in one direction alone, they might have grown accustomed to that in time, but that she was extravagant at times in the direction of opulence and then, quite as energetically, in that of shabbiness. Perhaps if she had appeared always in a temple sari of purple and orange, bordered with gold and green, and a blouse of corn yellow brocade, they would have accepted her extravagance. The trouble was that they were as often taken aback by seeing her in the garments of a demoralized washerwoman — so limp, so faded, so bedraggled and ragged were some of her cotton saris, in the shades of fawn and grey that female birds assume. So they never knew how, or what, to expect of her. There was something unnerving in it, they felt. Her husband, with a greater capacity for accommodation than most had — even in a society with a truly remarkable capacity for accommodation, as long as it made for comfort, for security, continuity and safety from change or scandal — had grown, over the years, immune to the shocks and suspicions she contrived to create. Yet now, having been separated from her for such a stretch, he was startled again by her appearance — she saw it on his face and was once again, maliciously amused.

'Why can't you just be neat and tidy?' he had asked despairingly in the beginning, but then learnt that these were the two qualities she had never known, and so she had continued to wear, instinctively, the garb of the male and then the female peacock. Now he said nothing — her dress was the least of his worries. Reaching down to unclasp his son's arms from his knees and lift him to his shoulder, he said gently, 'How are you?'

She stood back so that he could enter. As he did, she felt comfort, security, and dull, safe routine walk in, in quiet, grey strides. She remembered it was the second time he had come to fetch her from the island that he was always having to save her from the island. She felt so weak, she wanted to lay down her head and weep, 'My father's dead — look after me.' She cleared her throat. 'All right,' she said, hoarsely. From the corner of her eyes she saw Menaka, who had been leaning over the back of a chair, watching and smiling with a strangely sly, feline pleasure that made her quiver slightly, quietly slip away without saying a word to her father. Strange, Sita remarked in a bewildered stammer — why did she not come out?

'Your doctor phoned,' he said, sitting down with Karan on his lap. Karan pulled out a pen from his shirt pocket and demanded, 'Is this for me? Did you buy it for me? Can I have it?' Ignoring him, Raman said, 'She asked why you hadn't been coming to see her.'

'Oh what did you say?' Sita asked, entranced by the thought that there was someone, on the mainland, who remembered her, called her name, asked about her condition and future. She felt shaken, as by an unexpected love.

'Is it for me?' Karan clamoured, writing with the pen on the palm of his hand.

'I told her you'd gone away.'

'Yes,' she nodded and waited for him to say more. What had he said of the future? Nothing, apparently. He studied the pattern Karan had drawn on his hand and smiled into the boy's face.

'How are the boys?' she urged, hoarsely.

'Well,' he said.

Again she waited, clenching her hands, for something more — the news that they wanted her, missed her. Any news of them. How had she forgotten them for so long? Now all inside her clamoured for them, her sons. But he said nothing, kept his face averted from her, smiling into his son's spread fingers. Either he was tantalizing her, deliberately, or he had nothing more to give her, or he was just unaware of her needs and demands. He raised his hand and stroked Karan's hair with a gentleness she herself ached to attract, and she stared at him, bored into him with her eyes, wanting and not being given what she wanted.

Then why did you come? She wanted to shriek.

His head jerked, his hand fell to Karan's knee and he looked at her in astonishment. She had cried out aloud.

'Menaka called me,' he answered. He was sensible but not very sensitive and so told only the truth.

'Menaka called you?' she whipped around and was just in time to see Menaka's bare foot and the hem of her print frock disappear behind a pillar on the veranda — Menaka had been spying. For some reason she had slipped away and spied on this scene. Sita saw the reason now — Menaka had sent for her father. Menaka had betrayed her. 'Menaka! Why?'

Everyone around her winced — she saw them wincing at her harshness, her wildness that they so dreaded. But she could not stop herself now, not even for Karan's sake. Their betrayal had torn her open with such violence, now violence poured from her like blood. In it was also the shame, the disappointment: he had not come to see her, to fetch her, as she had supposed; he had come because Menaka had called him. He had betrayed her too. They had all betrayed her. Why?

'Papa, stick the pen in *my* pocket, Papa,' Karan begged.

He did so. 'The college admissions have begun,' he explained to her over the child's head. 'She wants to apply for admission to the Medical College. She has to appear for an interview. I've come to fetch her.'

She felt her jaw sagging far, far below, dangling foolishly in an empty space. 'She didn't tell me,' she muttered.

'She wrote...' he began patiently enough, then suddenly shrugged his shoulders and spoke more sharply. 'It's time for the admissions now. She mustn't miss the interview, sitting here on this island. She has to get back to her studies.'

'Ah!' she exclaimed with the very theatricality her husband feared, her children loathed and she could not control.

'Don't you *want* her to be a doctor?' he appealed with some desperation.

It was the wrong appeal. She only shook her head. He stared at her with distaste, thinking her grotesque. Her face was so grey, such sharp grooves ran from her nostrils to the corners of her mouth. It was the face of a woman unloved, a woman rejected. He shook his own head a little, with an equine movement — it was hard to believe now that he had married her, in a romantic whim, not only out of a cavalier's pity for a maiden's distress, but for her fire and beauty, her quite outstanding fire and beauty that he had recalled and gone over while sitting in the rocking boat, bowed to the pouring rain, while Moses pulled at the oars and pulled, carrying him to the island again.

But whereas her beauty had turned haggard through nerves and neglect, her fire had turned on him and even on the children, he felt, in spite and ill temper. He himself looked grey and lined and a backache still tormented him. How old they were, he thought, to be having another baby. They sat in the bare, grey room with the rain about them in a murky, wavering curtain and he thought they were too old and battered for it after all.

Karan shot out of his lap, bumping the top of his head against his father's lower lip, painfully. '*Khana's* come! *Khana's* come!' he shouted, capering with quite unaccustomed levity as Moses and Miriam entered in procession, carrying in dishes to set on the table, smiling the while with vermilion gums and ochre teeth, proud of the lunch they had prepared for the *Sahib* although they had never bothered to do much for merely the *Memsahib* and her children. There were shrimps, fried pink in butter, shredded cabbage and quartered muskmelons, sprinkled with lemon and sugar. They stood back, beaming, and watched as the family came up and scraped back their chairs and sat down.

Menaka slipped in, sliding silently on her bare feet, glancing from one parent to another. For all her guilt she could not quite suppress the jubilant upward quirk of triumph from the corners of her lips. Sita stared at her hostilely and twisted her own lips in bitterness. She was a traitor and Raman had come for her sake, not Sita's.

'You are cowards,' she murmured, dipping her head.

'Sita!' her husband warned. 'Let us have our lunch in peace,' he said, helping Karan to sit up to table and arranging his dishes for him.

Sita swung her head from side to side as if a spring had broken and it swung loose upon its hinge, and scattered the shredded salad all over her plate, not eating. Menaka nibbled, timidly watching her, but hungrily all the same. Karan was so astonished at the unusual opulence of the meal that he did not look up from his plate for the first ten minutes but ate with a concentration and a greed that his father noticed with distress. Only when the first helping had been cleared did he look up at his father again and think of other things.

'Papa, did you see my Dinky car?' he asked. 'Mama left it behind,' he accused her.

His father looked at him, smiling. 'I saw lots of them — they're all over the house. Every time I sat down hard on one or slipped on one and went sprawling, I thought of my son Karan.'

Karan ignored the sentimentality. 'No, no — the red one — the fire engine,' he insisted. 'I lost it, did you find it?'

Raman frowned and pretended to think hard. 'No, son, I can't remember.'

'I want it!' Karan suddenly bawled, letting his spoon drop with a clash. 'I want my fire engine.'

'I'll buy you one,' Raman said hastily. 'I'll buy you one as soon as we get to Bombay. I'll take you straight to the toy shop and you can buy one, two, *three* Dinky cars.'

Karan stopped bawling immediately and his voice sang. 'One, two, *three* Dinky cars!' he rejoiced, overcome. 'Straight to the toy shop for one, two, *three* Dinky cars!' Then he could not eat any more, jumped up and ran to the door. 'Let's go to Bombay,' he shouted, on fire to leave. 'Papa, I want to go to Bombay now.'

'Later, later,' Raman said, raising his eyes to Sita with a sly timidity that resembled Menaka's look. He had not wanted to bribe the child, as she plainly thought, had only not been able to restrain himself from offering the boy a gift, 'Come and have a piece of melon first. I won't buy you unless you eat your melon first,' he added with stern diplomacy.

At the first open mention of Bombay, even Menaka flowered. She dipped her long lashes and murmured, 'Have you seen Neera, Papa? Did you speak to Neera?'

'I see her everyday on the stairs when I go down to the car,' he told her, and began gossiping about the neighbours who lived in their block of flats, about their children, giving the messages they had sent to Menaka and Karan.

Sita watched, listened, bitterly and jealously. She marked their eagerness for the old routine, old friends, the city comforts and customs, and thought it treachery. She marked how they did not mention the island, had nothing to tell their father about it. Not even the jellyfish, she noted with anger. Not even the jellyfish. Or the cow drowned in the well. Or the crabs and shrimps brought in baskets — nothing. All that mattered to her, they discarded. Karan was going restive again.

'Will we go to Bombay now?'

'Later.'

'In two minutes?'

'No, later.'

'In ten minutes?'

'No, later.'

'Shall I count to hundered? After I've counted to hundered will we go?'

'For God's sake,' she broke out, 'don't start *counting*.'

Menaka rose and scraped back her chair, wiping her mouth and looping a strand of hair behind her ear, all in one rush. 'It's stopped raining — I'll take Karan out on the beach,' she said, as if trying of make up to her mother for her treachery.

'I don't want to go to the beach, I want to go to Bombay!' he began to howl, but she got him off the chair, drew him out of the room and hurried him away. Sita noticed the haste with which they ran from her. They had all got together, she decided, her family, to fight her, to reject her, to run away and hide from her. She went out on the terrace and watched their foreshortened figures rustle through the monsoon wilderness of the grove, their heads dip out of sight down the stone stairs beyond the casuarina fringe, then reappear on the dunes where the bindweed flowers were opening to the light of the still invisible sun, and disappear by the sea.

Raman followed her tiredly but resignedly — yet another responsibility to be shouldered. He sat down on the stone seat, unnaturally straight because of the backache that wracked him, but with his arms spread out along the wall and his head thrown back. Noting that unnatural posture — that desire to spread out and lie back, the will to remain upright, straight — she was moved despite all the treacheries and betrayals of the afternoon. It struck her then that he had suffered during these weeks that she had been away — had suffered from worry and anxiety about her, the unborn child, Menaka and Karan, living alone on the island in this wild season. His boys at home must have worried him too, while he was at work in the factory which was not without its problems, either — he never told her of them and she never gave much thought to it but the possibility struck her now. He looked worn, much older than his years. Nor could he stay here, resting, as she was doing.

He never hesitated — everything was so clear to him, and simple: life must be continued, and all its business — Menaka's admission to medical college gained, wife led to hosptial, new child safely brought forth, the children reared, the factory seen to, a salary earned, a salary spent. There was courage, she admitted to herself in shame, in getting on with such matters from which she herself squirmed away, dodged and ran. It took courage. That was why the children turned to him, sensing him to be the superior in courage, in leadership.

To certain people there comes a day
    When they must say the great Yes or the great No.
He who has the Yes ready within him
    reveals himself at once, and saying it crosses over
to the path of honour and his own conviction.

Then the pain of Menaka's betrayal and his own part in the conspiracy cut through her sharply and she reminded herself that she had courage, too, the courage of being a coward.

He who refuses des not repent. Should he be asked
    again, he would say No again. And yet that No —
the right No — crushes him for the rest of his life.

She had escaped from duties and responsibilities, from order and routine, from life and the city, to the unlivable island. She had refused to give birth to a child in a world not fit to receive the child. She had the imagination to offer it an alternative — a life unlived, a life bewitched. She had cried out her great 'No' but now the time had come for her epitaph to be written — *Che free per viltate il gran rifiute.* Very soon now that epitaph would have to be written.

And so, she felt, as she sat down beside him heavily, it was to be a battle between his brand of courage and her's. Or her cowardice and his. But a battle it would be.

She began. 'Menaka didn't tell me she had written to you. I didn't know anything about it.'

'There was nothing you could do for her on the island,' he explained reasonably — but kept his eyes averted. 'She had to tell me to send in her application form and see about her admission. She's so keen to join Medical College, Sita.'

'But it means leaving the island — going back!' she cried, spreading out her hands to show the loss of it.

He turned to stare at her, cautiously, watchfully. He seemed uncertain how she balanced — in what proportion her reason lay to her unreason. He seemed to have lost his knowledge of her, grown a little afraid, perhaps, of her excesses. He spoke very quietly, 'But you knew you must leave. You will have to come back.'

'I can't,' she pleaded, curling up her outspread hands, knotting them.

He heard the appeal in that negative. 'I've booked your room at the nursing home,' he said to make it easier.

'I can't' she repeated, 'go through it all over again.'

'You must,' he said, she shook her head. It seemed to her that he was always saying to her, 'You must. One must,' and that she was always shaking her head, crying, 'No, I can't.' The palm trees all shook their heads along with her, their leaves rustled one against the other, one saying 'You must', the other 'I can't', always producing that sound of battle, that sound of distress. They scraped against her, her skin peeled half away, bleeding, and yet they rubbed, scraped and fought.

A scream rang up, reeling out from the beach up to the knoll, and Sita leapt to her feet, shivering. It was Karan, tearing out scream upon scream, crying with that tearing, unappeasable sound, that primitive sound that pulled his mother to her feet in panic, brought her down the knoll at a run, in equal parts alarmed and outraged by the barbarity, the frenzy of that sound.

She ran, as clumsy now as an animal to whom this was alien pace — this rush. She heard Raman following, as clumsily, more slowly. He had been listening to such cries for years now, it was not to him that new, raw sound it was still to her ears. She had had so many children but never grown used to the alarm in that cry. Each time it tore a fresh gash in her. It made her wild, it made her run. Then to have another child, and hear it launch itself upon another scream.

When they came out on the dunes, they came within sight of the children playing in a rock pool. Karan had stopped crying. His cheeks glistening with wet, his lashes still stuck together with tears, he was lying comfortably enough on his stomach, dangling an arm into a shallow pool, amusing himself with an anemone. Menaka was standing beside him, her hands on her hips, poking at something in the pool with her toe. It was a scene of peaceful absorption. If it had recently been torn by shock or pain, there was no scar left of it, no mending left to be done.

The parents stopped on the dunes and did not approach or question them: even Sita had learnt enough to know there was no profit to be had from questioning the child now that he had forgotten, and so reopening the healed scar. They stood there limply together till they had stopped panting and got back their breaths. Then they trailed down the dunes and began to walk slowly and unevenly along the edge of the sea, she close enough to it to let the cream-frilled waves rush up and dash over her feet, then leave them washed and tingling on the glittering sand, and he a little more land-wards where the tide could not assault his shod feet, his dry dignity, and he could crunch along on the sand's white crust of littered shells. She stooped now and then to choose something from the flotsam scattered on the beach by last night's storm, regard it, caress it and then fling it extravagantly into the sea. He walked on heavily, as if pushing against the heavy, sodden monsoon air, avoiding the heaps of rotting weed, the sharp rocks about the small pools and the occasional rusted tin can.

She could see he took no pleasure in this walk. Well, she shrugged, he had not come to be with her or walk with her — he had come to fetch his daughter away. She twisted her lips for attack then. 'Go *back?*' she flung the question at him as if she were echoing something he had said. 'Go back and find it all the same — or worse? Rose fighting and screaming, the boys beating each other for fun, horrible things happening on the streets and in the flats all around us — everything so ugly and cruel? How can I?'

He bent his head lower, pushing back the wind that thrust at him, and looked stubborn, sullen. 'Other people put up with it — it's not so, so insufferable,' he said. 'Why can't you? Perhaps one should be grateful if life is only a matter of disappointment, not disaster.'

'Grateful for disappointments?' she was shocked, it was so abject, so negative, and she had thought him superior in courage. 'Put up with it? It would be cowardly to put up with it. And it isn't only I — there's the baby. That's what I refuse to do, you know — have it born to such, such a life.'

He sighed, stopped and for the first time, looked out to the sea that grew every moment more radiant as it reflected the brightening sky in which the clouds were parting to let through shafts of watery light. He said nothing, seemed unwilling to have the old, crazy arguments repeated all over again. He seemed to wish only to get on with it — take Menaka, take her back, resume the normal, everyday life of disappointments and anti-climaxes, and avoid disasters and climaxes. The littered beach, the stormy wind, she with her hair crazily flying — why did she not put it in a net or, at least, express annoyance at its disordering as another woman would? — all were obstacles he had to remove from his path so that he could proceed. But, for the moment, he looked too tired to move.

When he did at last speak she was taken aback for what he said was, 'Then are you always sad? Have you never been happy?' and looked at her at last with a shrouded, fearful look. For a moment she felt fluttering impulse to touch him and reassure him. Yes, yes, she ought to say as to a deeply distressed child, of course I am happy, we are happy, we will always be happy. But even to her children in distress she had not been able to say that. Even Menaka, then so small, in a white cotton nightgown, had sobbed, 'Will they put you in the ground when you die? Will they put you in the ground?' she had not been able to summon up and feed her any false reassurance. It simply did not exist for her and she could not make it exist. So she did not speak any words of love or reassurance to him. She looked away, staring at her feet, watching a frilled wave dash at her, sweep over her and then rush away.

Again and again the wave repeated its rush forward, its rush backward. Watching it, she saw again that point in time when she had realized what a farce marriage was, all human relationships were. It was the day she had admitted, out of a passion of boredom she could no longer contain and that burst, swamping her, that she was bored, bored. 'Bored'?' he had exclaimed, in genuine surprise. 'Why! How? With what?' and looked so puzzled, so pained. Then it was her turn to be puzzled and pained — she could not believe that he had really believed that all was well, not known that she was bored, dull, unhappy, frantic. She could hardly believe that although they lived so close together, he did not even know this basic fact of her existence.

Shaking her head, she admitted that she knew him little — for she had thought, seeing him spend his evenings and Sundays in that same chair, with that same sheet of newspaper, that — in his silence and gravity — he shared, to some extent, her distress at the tedium and ugliness of a meaningless life. Now, staring at his blank face, she realized it was not so, had not been so. He had not been distressed or dull. He was surprised to hear that she was. And she burst out laughing and laughed and laughed hysterically. Looking up from the swift, whispering rush and recession of the tedious waves, she saw again that puzzlement slowly working across the rigid map of his face. But she no longer felt like laughing. She lifted her hands to her head and pressed her hair flat against her temples. 'Do you know,' she said, 'in all these years we've lived together, in Bombay, I have known only one happy moment?'

She spoke so intensely, so vividly, he was obliged to ask 'When?' although he did not want to know, knew it would all be perverse.

'It was in the Hanging Gardens,' she recalled, slowly pacing beside him. 'One evening I took the children there. We were walking about. Near a tall hedge, on a bench, I saw a woman stretched out. A Muslim woman — she was wrapped up in her black *burkha*. Then she raised her veil and I saw her face. I saw her face lying in those black folds like a flower — a dead-white flower. Like a Persian lily, or tobacco flower at night. She was young. A very young woman, very, very pale and beautiful — beautiful,' she stammered, speaking faster and faster. 'Fatally anaemic — or fatally tubercular. Pale, you see, so white. Her head — this white, ill, beautiful head — lay in the lap of an old man. Much, much older than her. He had spectacles and a long grey beard. He looked down at her and caressed her face — so tenderly, so tenderly. I have never seen such tender, such gentle movements. And beside the bench, on the ground, two little girls were playing. Round little girls, rather dirty. Drawing lines in the gravel and staring at passers-by, staring at us. But the man and the woman never looked at anyone else, they looked at each other with such, such a strange, strange expression — I can't forget it. I can't explain it. Tender, loving, yes — but *inhumanly* so. I mean, one doesn't see such an expression on human faces ever. So intense. Quite divine — or insane. Why? I don't know, I've wondered. She was ill, dying perhaps. Perhaps she only had a short time to live. She was white as one dead, dead. He loved her — but who was he? Her father or husband? or a lover? I don't know. I watched them — I couldn't help myself — I felt as if I were gazing at a painting, or seeing a vision — and he kept caressing her face, and she lay still smiling. Once she raised her arms a little, laughing. Then I caught the children by their hands and we went away — I wanted them to be private, alone. No one to see or touch them. They were like a work of art — so apart from the rest of us. They were not like us — they were inhuman, divine. So strange — that love, that sadness, not like anything I've seen or known. They were so white, so radiant, they made me see my own life like a shadow, absolutely flat, uncoloured. That, that was the only — the only happy...' she stammered to a close, holding her hair about her face, and she looked as if the normal covering of her face had been stripped off her bones, leaving such bare agony as he could not bear to look at.

Turning away, he said, 'And *that* was the only happy moment of your life?' It seemed then that the ordinary disappointments of his life were indeed turning to disaster.

She walked on and sighed. 'Yes, I think I used to have glimpses like that — like that one when I lived here before, on this island. There used to be some magic here, too. But it went. As I was growing up and my father old, it went. It's gone. And it was of a darker kind, murkier — not pure like that, not dazzling.'

He suddenly thrashed his arms against his sides, like a large, grey bird in despair. 'Any woman — any one would think you inhuman. You have four children. You have lived comfortably, always, in my house. You've not had worries. Yet your happiest memory is not of your children or your home but of strangers, seen for a moment, some lovers in a park. Not even of your own children.'

'Children?' she murmured, distractedly. 'Children only mean anxiety, concern — pessimism. Not happiness. What other women call happiness is just — just sentimentality.'

'Sentimentality!' he shot out. 'If only you were, if you could be a little more sentimental, you would be more human. And how can you call someone else's happiness, seen in a park, for a moment, *your* happiest memory? I don't understand.'

'Perhaps that's not the word for it after all,' she agreed. 'It is the wrong word. But you see, that was the only time I've ever seen that life has meaning. I thought my father's did — and then it turned out it didn't. And, normally, for all of us, everyone I know it has *none.* But *their* lives seemed to have one — if not meaning, then a secret, a strange divine secret,' she concluded, and seemed pleased to have been able to explain it to herself, even if not to him. 'But then,' she added, 'it all became harder than ever before, for me. Very hard — this making of compromises when one didn't want to compromise, when one wanted to — to...'

'But we went through harder times — in the beginning,' he cried suddenly. 'We got through them, didn't we?'

'In those days,' she explained, 'I thought I could live with you and travel alone — mentally, emotionally. But, after that day, that wasn't enough. I had to stay whole, I *had* to. Do you know,' she added hesitantly, 'I think perhaps that is the urge my mother felt when she ran away to Benares. But what happened to her? I wonder, Raman. I had to run away, too — to the island.'

'You're both deserters then, you mean?' he asked tersely, not without scorn.

'No, no — desertion, that's cowardly. I wasn't doing anything cowardly,' she begged him to see, with a turbulence of pride. 'I was saying No — but positively, *positively* saying No. There must be some who say No, Raman!'

He pretended a laugh. It was grotesquely distorted.

'Oh,' she said, muddling her hair with her hands, muddling the sand with her feet, suddenly anxious to close this conversation and resume the silence of the past. 'Perhaps I never ran away at all. Perhaps I am only like the jellyfish washed up by the waves, stranded there on the sand bar. I was just stranded here by the sea, that's all. I hadn't much to do with it at all,' she sadly admitted, with that black, stripped truthfulness that she could never colour or coat.

'So you're no more than a jellyfish,' he said bitterly. 'You call yourself a helpless jellyfish. Yet see what you have done to yourself, to all of us.'

'All of you?' she vaguely asked. 'But you have nothing to do with it. Nothing. There's just the sea — it drowns us or strands us on the sand-bar — and there's the island. That's all.'

'Then,' he said, 'I'll go now,' and turned and started to walk up the beach. From the way he turned, the way he disregarded her, did not see if she followed or not, she felt him release her then — give her up. She felt it as surely as if his hand, till now clutching her hand, had let it drop, let her go. He did it not in a passion, but out of pure weariness with her, weariness with her muddle, her dark, muddled drama. He had no part in it, she had said, so he could leave her to it. He released her and at last she was free.

She stood still, straddling the line where the water met the sand, clashed and separated, and felt herself released and freed. Immensely tired now, all emptied out, the drama drained, the passion crumpled, she felt so light that she could have risen and floated out to sea, a black sea-bird. But she did not. The wind jumped up and buffeted her so that she could not stand still and she began to trail after him, knowing she would follow him, follow the trail of footprints he had laid out for her. Like the freed sea-bird at evening, she wheeled around and began to circle about and then dropped lower and lower towards her home.

She lowered her head and searched out his footprints so that she could place her feet in them, as a kind of game to make walking back easier, and so her footprints, mingled with his, sometimes accurately and sometimes not, made a chain of links, wet and muddy hollows, across the washed and brushed sand. Seeing one footprint follow another so precisely, so logically, words, too, sorted themselves out, formed lines, and she recalled the entire verse she had so long been pursuing:

The wild young heifer, glancing distraught,
    With a strange, new knocking of life at her side
Runs seeking a loneliness.
    The little grain draws down the earth, to hide
Nay, even the slumbrous egg as it labours
    under the shell
Patiently to divide and sub-divide,
    Asks to be hidden, and wishes nothing to tell.

Jerking her head up, she wanted to shout to him, 'Wait! I'll explain — I can explain everything now,' and the words of explanation clamoured inside her mouth. The heifer, the grain, the slumbrous egg and she herself. 'The strange, new knocking of life at her side. ... Asks to be hidden and wishes nothing to tell.' She wanted to shout the lines to him, repeat it all to him. She felt that if she could bring herself to tell him how the lines had haunted her, how this poem by Lawrence clarified it all for her, and how and why she had searched for it and only now remembered it, then the great gap between them would be newly and securely bridged.

But, as she caught up with him, panting, he spoke first, in a quite normal, even voice, of some quite different emotion. 'It wouldn't be bad,' he said, 'to give up the factory and come to live here. Do some farming. I'd like that. But what can you farm here? Bombay duck! That stinks even worse than the factory,' he laughed.

She laughed too, gulping down the words of explanation, the poem, in painful swallows. She thought how nice he really was, how much the nicest man she knew. She allowed him, then, to have his triumph, not to try to cap it with her verse. He deserved that triumph, purely by being so unconscious of it, so oblivious.

Together they walked up the stone steps to the grove. There, on the top step, she stopped to catch her breath, saw again the frayed rope dangling from the old fig tree like a hanged ghost, saw a nettled moth sail out of the weeds into the evening air, saw the windowpanes of the house on the knoll lit by the setting sun to a mysterious brilliance so that the house seemed like a trick constructed of mirrors and the moment for telling him was quite over. It might come up again, another time, but she did not really believe it would. It was over.

He strode on, hurried and vigorous, calling to Menaka who stood waiting for them on the terrace, biting a finger worriedly, looking a very young child again in that attitude.

'Pack up your things, Menaka,' he called to her, 'we're going now, before it's dark.'

Behind him, Sita shouted, 'Don't worry, Menaka, I will pack. I will pack all our things together.'

Menaka flew into the house shouting, 'Karan! Karan! Karan!'

As she knelt beside the open suitcase, and the children ran back and forth, bringing her their things to put in, she felt — tired, dishevelled and vacant as she was — like a player at the end of the performance, clearing the stage, picking the costumes, in equal parts saddened and relieved. Her time on the island had been very much of an episode on a stage, illuminated by gaudy sunset effects and played to thunderous storm music. The storm ended, the play over, the stage had now to be cleared — then the players could go home. Instead of being a person who for many years had had to perform on a false stage and had only here, on the island, begun to live a life of primitive reality, she had actually been playing the part here of an actress in a theatrical performance and was now to return to a life of retirement, off-stage.

But was she sure it was not the other way around after all? Had not her married years, her dulled years, been the false life, the life of pretence and performance and only the escape back to the past, to the island, been the one sincere and truthful act of her life, the only one not false and staged?

How could she tell, how decide? Which half of her life was real and which unreal? Which of her selves was true, which false? All she knew was that there were two periods of her life, each in direct opposition to the other. Confused, she begged the jumping, whirling children, 'Go out. Go out to your father. Let me finish the packing alone.' She shook her head angrily at the confusion, the muddle of it all. Neither sea nor sky were separate or contained — they rushed into each other in a rush of light and shade, impossible to disentangle.

She rolled up vests and folded shirts and, laying them side by side and one on top of the other, it occurred to her that as soon as she got home she would have to begin to get together, then pack a suitcase full of infant's garments. Through her mind flowed a white, flapping succession of nappies, vests, and something quite extraordinary called 'booties' that would have to be gathered together. She could see the expressionless faces of the night nurses in the gynae ward as they leant against the wall, one white-shod foot up against the plaster, in the greenish night light, regarding her as she came in, ravaged by the first pains. She could see their considering faces as they unpacked and carried off the garments to the nursery — with approval or disdain, would it be? She could see the impassive face of nurses who would stay by her in the theatre, now and then glancing at her large, flat watch, bored by yet another woman's panic-stricken labour.

Then, once the infant was born, she would faintly shrug, slightly toss her head, a gesture at once of tiredness and relief, and turn to the doctor, noisily washing at the sink, and chaff her for a moment or two, taking this small interval of relaxation as she might get a cup of tea, for refreshment, although the doctor, more exhausted, would scarcely reciprocate — between two and five in the morning, humanity is hardly possible. Sita would lie as still as though paralysed in a fearful accident, with blue lips and a grey sensation of death. She found herself imitating, in self-defence, that nurse in advance — that faint shrug, that slight toss of the head, and even her voice relaxed as she called, 'Karan, shall I pack any shells or things for you?'

'No!' he promptly shouted back, and she got to her feet and looked out of the window to see him running round and round in circles on the terrace, as if warming up his motor for the journey. Giddy from kneeling and bending so long, she felt herself whirling round and round as well. She felt the long, straight, monotonous track of her life whip itself round her in swift circles, perhaps a spiral, whirling around and around till its very lines dissolved and turned to a blur of silver, the blurred silver of the mirror-like windowpanes. All was bright, all was blurred, all was in a whirl. Life had no periods, no stretches. It simply swirled around, muddling and confusing, leading nowhere.

Raman got up from the stone seat. 'Ready?' he asked.

She nodded. The children shrieked and flew down the knoll to the bullock cart that waited under the palms. Moses was waving his whip over the bullocks' horns, uttering grunts of admonishment. Miriam came screaming out of her hut to seize and smack her Karan-baba once again but he hastily scrambled up into the cart, out of her reach. Sita got in, then Raman. The bullock cart set off, rattling over the ruts in the road, and all the palm trees shivered.

When the car had driven off, Moses did not get back into the boat immediately. Wiping the perspiration off his face with his fingers, he loosened the *lungi* about his hips and shuffled into the tea-shop. There was no one there but Jamila who stood in the doorway, watching. She laughed to see him come, with a round twist of her belly.

He glared. 'Get me a glass of *kaju,* quick,' he growled.

'Got you pay, eh, Moses? Paid you well, did she, Moses?' Jamila cackled as she led him into the backroom where her husband sat slouched on a tin chair, drinking Jamila's thick yellow brew. 'Moses has been paid off,' she shrieked, and poured him a glass. A cloud seemed to rise from it, of steam or stench.

'I'm still the watchman,' Moses shouted, angered by her cawing and cackling.

'*Whose* watchman? She's not coming back, is she? Your *Memsahib's* flown, Moses.' Jamila's belly shook with a big laugh.

'She'll come back,' grumbled Moses. 'The *Sahib* said they would come in winter, for the holidays.'

Jamila sneered. 'Never. She's seen what her house looks like now — out on your Manori. She didn't like it much, did she?'

'It's hard,' her husband spoke up from his corner. One hand inside his shirt, he sat massaging his thin, sick chest. 'On the island, life is hard. No taps, no electricity, no market, no company. It's hard.'

'She's had enough. She's gone, Moses, she won't come back,' Jamila teased.

Moses glared at her with yellow eyes, sullenly. Then, majestically, he said, 'The house is still there. The well is there. The coconut trees are there, and the *cheekoo* trees. What do we want her there for? After all, she — she is not like her father.'

Jamila suddenly ceased to laugh and tease. She looked depressed as she slumped down at the table and poured herself a drink. 'Not like him,' she gloomily agreed. 'She — she looks *plain.* A plain woman. Nobody. Not like her father. *That* was a man,' she smacked her lips appreciatively.

Her husband suddenly sang out in a quaver. 'He was like a god — a magic man.'

'Magic,' agreed Jamila, rolling her tongue inside her mouth. 'He did magic.'

'Who can forget?' Moses suddenly thundered, scowling at his audience of two.

'No one, no one,' the sick man cooed, calming him. 'But *she* —,' Jamila spat, 'she was plain. Not like him. Too plain, Moses.'

'Mad too,' he contemptuously growled. 'Mad. One day Miriam saw her sitting on the floor, playing with mud. Like a dirty brat. Playing with mud! An old woman like that! Mad.'

'*Vah!*' cried Jamila in wonder, then doubled up with laughter. Pressing her hand over her mouth, her laughter burst out in bubbles of spit. 'Playing in the mud,' she gasped. 'That old, plain woman?'

'She was mad,' Moses explained. 'Got angry, too, just like that, for nothing, all the time.' He drank deeply and shook his head as if a fly bothered him. 'So angry always. Angry with me, angry with Miriam, angry because it rained, angry because there was no food — *always* angry. Mad people are like that. Huh,' he spat out a hiccup. 'Let her go. Who cares? We will only remember *him,* the father. How he lived, and his magic. The island is his, it is really his.'

'Still it is his,' the sick man agreed in a quaver.

'Who is she to come here to live?' Jamila demanded. 'Let her go.'

'Let her go,' Moses growled, and they all dipped their heads and drank. It was so dark in the backroom, so dark and hot, they could see scarcely anything at all. But soon others — from the island, from the mainland — began to come in for a drink.

❑❑❑